JONAH AND SARAH

The Library of Modern Jewish Literature

JONAH AND SARAH

JEWISH STORIES OF RUSSIA AND AMERICA

DAVID SHRAYER-PETROV

Edited by Maxim D. Shrayer

Syracuse University Press

First Edition 2003
03 04 05 06 07 08   6 5 4 3 2 1

The short stories published in this collection are works of fiction. Names, characters, places, and incidents either are the product of the author's imagination or are used fictitiously, and any resemblance to actual persons living or dead, or to actual locations, is entirely coincidental.

The paper used in this publication meets the minimum requirements of American National Standard for Information Sciences—Permanence of Paper for Printed Library Materials, ANSI Z39.48–1984.∞™

Library of Congress Cataloging-in-Publication Data
Shraer-Petrov, David.
[Short stories. English. Selections]
Jonah and Sarah : Jewish stories of Russia and America / David Shrayer-Petrov; edited by Maxim D. Shrayer.— 1st ed.
p. cm.—(The library of modern Jewish literature)
Includes bibliographical references.
ISBN 0–8156–0764–4 (alk. paper)
1. Jews—Fiction. I. Shrayer, Maxim, 1967– II. Title. III. Series.
PG3549.S537 A2 2003
891.73'44—dc21   2003009848

Manufactured in the United States of America

CONTENTS

David Shrayer-Petrov was born in 1936 in Leningrad, Russia, and debuted as a poet in the 1950s. After studying medicine, Shrayer-Petrov served as a military physician in Belorussia before returning to Leningrad to pursue both literature and medicine. He married Emilia Polyak in 1962. The couple moved to Moscow, where their son Maxim was born and Shrayer-Petrov's first collection of verse came out in 1967. Literary exploration of Jewish themes put Shrayer-Petrov in conflict with the Soviet authorities, limiting publication of his work and prompting him to emigrate. Instead of granting him an exit visa, the Soviet authorities launched a campaign of persecution and ostracism that cost Shrayer-Petrov his medical position and membership in the Union of Soviet Writers and culminated in arrests by the KGB. A Jewish refusenik from 1979 to 1987, Shrayer-Petrov lived as an outcast in his native country but continued to write; over his last decade in Russia he wrote two novels, several plays, a memoir, and many stories and verses. He finally left the USSR in 1987, settling in Providence, Rhode Island. His arrival in the West brought forth a flow of publications, including six collections of poetry, three novels, two volumes of memoirs, and many contributions to literary magazines in Europe and North America. In 1992 Shrayer-Petrov's novel *Herbert and Nelly* was nominated for the Russian Booker Prize. Dr. Shrayer-Petrov divides his time between writing and doing cancer research at Brown University. The latest among his sixteen books are the novel *Töstemaa Castle* (2001) and the poetry collection *Form of Love* (2003).

Maxim D. Shrayer, the author's son and editor and cotranslator of the present collection, was born in 1967 in Moscow and emigrated to the United States in 1987. He is professor of Russian and English at Boston College. Among Shrayer's books are *The World of Nabokov's Stories* and *Russian Poet/Soviet Jew.* He is the editor of the forthcoming two-volume *Anthology of Jewish-Russian Literature, 1800–2000.*

ACKNOWLEDGMENTS

We would like to thank all the contributing translators for creating faithful English versions of the Russian originals.

We thank the editors of the Russian- and English-language periodicals where these stories appeared in the original and in translation.

Our special gratitude extends to the entire staff of Syracuse University Press for their perfectionism, patience, and enthusiasm.

Ken Frieden read an earlier version of the manuscript and made very helpful suggestions.

Christopher Springer read and gently critiqued drafts of over half of the translations included in this book.

Stephen Vedder and Michael S. Swanson of Boston College Media Service have done a stellar job with the jacket photos. Peter Rahaghi, a diligent assistant, proofread the entire manuscript.

Michael Keith, a colleague and a fellow author, has been a great friend and supporter of this collection, and "that bottle of Moët et Chandon" is waiting for him to be opened on the day of publication.

Emilia Shrayer and Karen Lasser read the manuscript several times and offered invaluable comments. No words can express our gratitude and love.

D.S.-P. and M.D.S.

PREFACE
To Be Ripped Away

These thirteen stories bear testimony to more than sixteen years of setting roots in my new country. Almost half of them were written before June 7, 1987, when my family and I left the Soviet Union. The other stories in this collection have been composed on route or after coming to America. Whether they feature characters still living in the old country or having already arrived in the New World, these stories are a record of a Jewish writer's separation from his Russian homeland.

꧁꧂

When did this happen finally? This break, this cutting of the umbilical cord through which my love for Russia had been nourished? Now it's a done deal, irrevocable. I'm ripped away forever, a child of incidental passion—certainly not of purchased love. How did it happen that my forefathers came to love this land? Did she love them back? Torn away, I bleed; having cast me away, Russia is bleeding too, because we still share the same blood flow—the Russian language.

Maybe this ripping away began in my post-siege childhood, when we—hungry boys from the Vyborg working-class district of Leningrad—devised a new way of procuring food. Across the road from our house, a bread factory worked day and night. The pregnant scent of bread stupefied us. All day, day after day, we would think of nothing but bread. Especially in the summer, when there was nothing to do but dream of food. The chimney of the bread factory, with its dark gray cloud of smoke, was for us a symbol of happiness realized. We elaborated on our plans, incredible in their boldness and cunning, for procuring the steaming golden loaves that lay in a row behind the windows of the bread factory, blazing with sweetness and plenty.

And so, one day, one of us figured out how to get the loaves. We bent iron rods into long hooks. Inside the bread factory it was hot. We knew this because the women worked with only robes covering their naked bodies. When the robes fell open, the rosy, fattened bodies of the female workers taunted us just like the golden bodies of the loaves. It was hot, and the women would open the windows from inside. Outside, on the street, we would roam, hungry. On the windows hung iron prison grates, made of the same kind of bars as our hooks. On purpose or by chance, the women would put the fresh steaming loaves on the windowsills. Surely not for us, but for themselves; it's impossible to eat oven-hot loaves, so they cooled them by the open windows, guarded by grates.

One of us—we took turns procuring the daily bread—would step up alone to one of the open windows, the one where a loaf lay cooling, push the hook through a square in the grate, drive the hook into the loaf, then, with a lightning jerk, pull out the golden steaming body of the loaf, and, hiding it under his jacket, rush across the street to the park. There we shared the booty. Like the rest of the urchins, I would pull out a loaf when my turn came. We were always lucky, to the point where it seemed the women were intentionally opening windows and putting out bread for us.

But one day, when I pushed the hook through the grate and pierced the loaf, I felt a tug: someone had seized the hook and was pulling me to the window. I looked inside. A portly young woman stood by the windowsill. Her red hair was hidden under a gauze kerchief, but its fierceness burst through. A golden halo glowed around the kerchief. The redhead woman was clothed in a white sleeveless robe. As a result of the tense struggle for the hook, the right side of the robe slipped down, and a breast burst through. Her armpit was ablaze with red curly hair. I let go of the hook, and stared, wide-eyed, at this beautiful sight. Too bad the boys weren't there. They were waiting for me in the park.

"And just what are you up to?" the redhead spoke up. "Our *Russian* kids, you know, have been going hungry forever. And you *kikes,* you think you're not getting enough bread?"

Dumfounded, I fell silent in defeat.

"Here, little Jew, eat. Don't matter to me. It's government bread." The redhead pushed a snout of bread through a hole in the grate, and then tossed my iron hook into the street.

I was nine years old at the time. Probably I hadn't yet learned to make the right decision at a moment's notice. Or maybe I hadn't learned to coordinate my natural conduct with the specific rules of the game. I still haven't learned that, by the way. But back then I wasn't thinking of anything like that. I grabbed the loaf, hid it under my jacket—in case I ran into a cop—and, waving the hook victoriously, raced to the park. There, in the clearing, at the foot of a big fat oak, the neighborhood boys were waiting for me to return with the booty. We divided up the loaf and began to eat it. Then I felt nauseous. The weight rose up in my stomach and chest, the blood started pounding in my temples, and I ran off into the hawthorn bushes . . .

ᏯᎻᏬᎧ

The condition of morbid exceptionality began to pursue me. I hadn't noticed it before, apparently. In the same way, a girl is oblivious to her lack of beauty until she enters the field of vision of strangers, on the pole of choice. She hasn't been chosen. Or the opposite: they chose her so as to exclude her from the game. More and more, the other boys marked me out. In all likelihood, growing up I came to look more and more Jewish. As children, Jews are often blond and blue-eyed. It is hard to tell a Jewish child from Slavic children. Then, around the time of puberty, Semitic (Mediterranean) features express themselves. Perhaps this has something to do with the origin of the Jewish people: did the original Caucasian type mingle with the nomadic tribes of Arabia?

I started taking heed of chance conversations: in school, while riding the streetcar, at the store. Even a slight hint at my non-Slavic, Jewish origins wounded my pride. I assumed the role of the one being chased and hunted. This gave birth to a keen sense of compassion for other persecuted and misfortunate: cripples, prisoners of war, holy fools, orphans, Gypsies. I pursued friendships with those peers who also had some kind of abnormality: in the family, in the body, in the heart. I became aggressive towards the successful ones.

I had a best friend: the illegitimate son of a Jew and a village girl who had come from Luga to Leningrad before the war in order to find work. Together, like two young wolves, we scoured the provincial little streets and the overgrown parks of the Vyborg district. We thirsted for fights, where we could wash away the shame of our exceptionality in pain and blood. We feared nothing. Our poor mothers!

One day, when we were fourteen or fifteen, around 1949 or '50, we went to a dance at an all-girls school. In those days, boys and girls went to separate schools. I think it was January, winter break, a New Year event, just a few days after the holiday itself. The school was three streetcar stops away from my house toward to the center of Leningrad, past the Forestry Academy park. We put on clean shirts, flared trousers, jackets with inlaid geometric shapes in dark coarse cloth. We pulled on our coats and hats. The streetcar chugged along so slowly, and our souls flew so impetuously, to the dwelling-place of airy smiling creatures with unearthly shapes that we could approach, perhaps even touch, when dancing.

And so we danced, we went to smoke in the bathroom assigned to the boys, and again wandered around the dance hall or stood against the walls and looked for the most beautiful of these fairytale creatures they called "girls," a liquid and tender name, like dragonfly wings. We finally picked one of them and called her "our girl." We even invited her to dance once or twice. We believed that this girl, with a pale and tender face, already mature-looking because of the sharply outlined lips and the huge, violet eyes, we believed she would also see herself as *our girl,* and got mad, though truly, not for long and not at her, when she danced with someone else. But even while dancing with another, *our girl* managed to cast a violet glance around the room and see us, and smile at us in a barely perceptible way. That meant the game was still going on, and while according to the rules of the game we were obliged to part with her, this was not for long; as in all games, this parting was not serious. The serious thing was this: she was *our girl.* All the boys saw this and did not venture to ask her more than once in the evening. We were happy in our sense of connection with this wonderful girl.

In the middle of the evening, when we finally decided that no danger would threaten our future friendship with the possessor of the violet eyes, my friend nudged me with his elbow.

"Look! No way out of a fight. Soplov is hooked on *our girl.*"

Soplov was the son of some Party official or other. The phonograph was playing, the records emitted foxtrots and tangos into the hall, and we already knew too well that we were in for a fight. I went up to Soplov, who, even after the second dance with *our girl* had not stepped aside; rather, he was holding her hand, indicating his intention to ask her again. I thought she looked frightened. Of course, I decided, she's just afraid of Soplov. It was dangerous to turn down that type of person. The boys said that he never went anywhere without his Finnish blade.

"Get lost," I told Soplov tersely and rudely, and my friend nodded, affirming my words. Soplov, of course, knew us both, knew of our fame as despairing fighters for truth, knew that we had never relented in an honest battle. But the girl was so beautiful, she looked with such interest at the boys all ready to tear each other to shreds on her account, that for Soplov to give in to us, playing the coward, would mean losing her forever. And he was used to losing nothing.

"You two get the hell of here! Go back to your Palestine," Soplov said loudly, still holding *our girl* tightly by the hand.

"Palestinians" were what they called Jews in those years. We both hit Soplov at once. I dealt him a blow in the right socket, in the very corner, where the red fleshy triangle of the tear canal is exposed. My friend hit him on the left, on the lower jaw, still hanging a little from the last sounds of the foul sentence rolling down in his poisonous saliva. Soplov collapsed. We had to make it to the cloakroom before the chaperoning teachers called the cops. The most important thing was to hide from law enforcement; otherwise there would be a trial and penal colony. For some reason I used to connect the frightening word "colony" with my grandfather's stories of how his father, my great-grandfather, had escaped from czarist authorities that wanted to draft him at a young age into years of military service.

A signal system, unknown to us, must have been at work, because as soon as we jumped out into the street, the cops flew behind us in their "striped tube" howling and snorting, up to the entrance of the school.

"The park! Faster!" my friend cried.

We hurled ourselves in the direction of the park. The running was hard. The raw January wind, hard as ice in the -15°F frost, cut the face and squeezed the lungs. We stole through courtyards, along

Lesnoy Prospekt. "Colony, colony," the cops' sirens were howling. We ran up to a bridge over the streetcar tracks. Beyond the bridge was the safety of a park. We heard a dog barking.

"German shepherds. Let's go for the tree nursery," I said, tugging my friend's sleeve.

Through a tall fence, ensnared at the top with barbed wire, we crossed to the nursery. We heard the chase go off to the right.

We came home late at night. Tear-streaked, my mother told me that the cops had come to see her. They were looking for me and my friend. We lived in the same building, on the same floor. Aunt Lyuba, my friend's mother, wrote a statement saying that we were at her father's in the country and had left before New Year's. And our neighbors signed the false statement. On the six A.M. train we fled from Leningrad to my friend's grandfather's house in the village, on the Oredezh river. "From colony to Palestine," joked grandfather, formerly a coachman in prerevolutionary St. Petersburg.

ᏮᎥᎥᎥᎧ

One can write a whole book: a story of injuries, great and small, brought on by intent or chance, by strangers and those who seemed to be friends, at work, at the stadium, in the metro, at the restaurant table. Often I forgot about the injuries, especially when I found myself among equals, when I experienced burdens equal to theirs: in the army, on expeditions, in moments of danger. All the more horrible was the sudden return to the alienating sense of inferiority.

After Medical School I served in the army. It was the second year of my career as a lieutenant in the medical corps. Following a two-week leave, I returned to Borisov, a Belorussian town where my tank division was stationed. I had visited Leningrad; my mother, friends, and I had discovered calm. After my vacation, after relaxed meals, the Leningrad theaters, bridges and embankments, after civilian clothes, in which you may choose not to salute an officer wearing more stars than yourself, after all this, the return to service was oppressive.

They announced to us that we were going for exercises. The change of scene before us seemed like a breath of fresh air: to leave the drugstore tedium of a provincial army town with its sickeningly straight rows of pill-boxes. And so it was: we were awaited by deserted fields of wheat. Cornflowers bloomed through the gold and ochre of the straw. Thousands of starlings feasted in the abandoned fields, collecting fallen grain.

Our unit set up camp at the edge of the forest, between fields and a village. In the evenings, the officers found diversion in the local dance club and had flings with sharp-tongued girls of Polish stock, often encountered in villages of western Belorussia. During the day there were firing drills, and in the evenings our brotherhood of officers came up with new amusements: horseback riding, fishing, cards.

One of the officers, a senior lieutenant who served in the army headquarters, brought hunting gear along to the training. He knew the point of entertainment and had the reputation of a first-class wit and a ladies' man.

"Fish get tiresome," he told us, referring to the dance parties at the local club. "And in order to eat this peasant fish with pleasure, we need a change."

We decided to treat ourselves to game. We went to distant fields to shoot starlings. There were three of us: the *shtabnik* (the officer from the headquarters), a tall fellow from the Kuban region in the south of Russia, with wavy glossy hair and a thread-fine mustache; the division chemist, a captain in his forties, originally from outside Tula (this gave him grounds for drunken hinting at a possible relation with Lev Tolstoy); and myself, a lieutenant, a physician. The *shtabnik* gave us rifles. We went up to the flock of feasting birds from the direction of the sun, which was slowly dropping past the horizon. The *shtabnik* bared his teeth, squatted, and uttered some un-Russian robbers' whistle. His ancestor, a Cossack chieftain, probably used this whistle to warn his men of danger. The brown masses of starlings grew tense. The field resounded with the flapping of a thousand pairs of wings, with hubbub and cries.

"Fire!" shouted the *shtabnik* and fired.

I also fired. Then the division chemist. Arrested in flight by deathly pellets, the bodies of starlings fell like stones to the ground. The shtabnik, in the savage heat of the hunt, fired from the shotgun at the fleeting remainder of the flock. Once again, stones pelted down from the sky. We rushed to pick up the starlings, and brought our booty to camp.

In two hours the soldier-cook came and called us to dinner. This cook was in his first year of service. He had been drafted from a small Ukrainian town—formerly a shtetl—near Vinnitsa, I think Khmelnik. But I remember that he was terribly shy by nature, and his shyness was especially exacerbated by the fact that he misrolled and lisped many of the Russian consonants. A sweet waft of smoke was circling over the cauldron. We poured vodka into mugs. The cook bent over the cauldron and fished out the potatoes, stewed along with the game.

"Damn tasty," remarked the division chemist, happily sucking on the bird's bones.

The cook took a seat a few steps to the side. You could hear him puffing over his bowl.

"Hey, what kind of bird is this?" our *shtabnik* burst out, interrupting the feast. "Get over here, you cretin!"

The cook approached. He hadn't managed to wipe the potato from his mouth, and the brown remains of food blended with the red fatty freckles on his face. He glanced timidly at the officer, blinking his short pale lashes. I got disgusted, and pushed my bowl aside, staring at the *shtabnik* and the cook. The *shtabnik* held between index finger and thumb a starling that was cooked but not plucked. It was strange to see this dead bird, resembling a stuffed animal, amid the meat and potato that had lost their forms and turned into a food product.

"So, you rot, have you desired to make fools of Russian officers?" The *shtabnik* rose. Scanning his surroundings with bloodshot eyes, he saw an iron rod, which the cook had been using as a poker, to stir the coals under the cauldron.

"Fohgive me, comhade senioh lieutenant," the frightened cook said, stepping backward.

We had no time to come to our senses when the *shtabnik* skewered his ill-fated unplucked starling on the rod and smeared it across the soldier's face: "You stinking kike! I'll teach you to cheat Russian officers!"

The cook trembled with fear and hurt. The division chemist muttered, while still chewing his food: "Come on, brothers. These things happen. Why aggravate yourselves?"

I couldn't hold back any longer. I had to run into the forest, to the river, under the train rumbling in the distance. Or take revenge. I wrested the rod from the *shtabnik*'s hand. With the left hand I struck him in the plexus, and when he, shrunken, bared his fine-mustached face, all wild with rage and pain, I dealt him a blow with the rod, slashing his cheek, just as his own Cossack grandfathers used to slash the unarmed students, workers, and Jews.

"You want a court martial? You Jew-defender!" the *shtabnik* croaked, hunching over and covering the deep cut on his cheek.

But the charges weren't pressed for some reason. Nothing came of this incident and soon I got an honorable discharge.

⟨⟩

When the Nazis broke into the house of my grandfather, an old rabbi, he was bending over the sacred books with a *talles* over his shoulders, swaying, like a Bedouin, reading the sacred book of the desert with the verses of the oases, the rhymes of springs and the refrains of sandstone hills. The Nazis shot the old Jew; as for the sacred books, they trampled on them and burned them.

There exists in the world a saving proportionality. Not a harmony in the grand poetic sense of the word, but a proportionality, intended for the purpose of distributing happiness and unhappiness among people. I've learned this from my modest experience. A writer has no way of knowing this for certain, except in the depths of his own soul. Where else, if not in these inescapable depths, is a writer to find a knowledge of man? Of course experience, observation, imagination are important. All these are forms, into which the energy of the writer's soul is poured. And the more actively this soul lives in the outer and inner world, the more possibilities the writer has of understanding his heroes, of penetrating, along with them, into the secrets of their soul, of living their happy and bitter moments along with them. The right hand of fate has been raised over the head of the hero, while he, unaware of this, lives as if he had a thousand years of rejoicing and happiness ahead.

Providence, Rhode Island   D.S.-P.
June 2002

Translated from the Russian by Diana Senechal and Maxim D. Shrayer

Composed in 1979 and considerably reworked in the early 1990s, "To Be Ripped Away" (Ottorzhenie) appeared in the New York Jewish weekly *Evreiskii mir* (Jewish world) 31 (8 November 1996). For inclusion in this collection, the author revised "To Be Ripped Away" and added a new section, and it appears for the first time in English.

JONAH AND SARAH

APPLE CIDER VINEGAR

Last fall I went to the Tishinsky farmers' market for apples. There were several markets in Moscow that I loved. There was the Leningradsky—solid and reliable, with stable prices, where you could always find homemade cottage cheese, crunchy pickles, and magnificent carnations; the Koptevsky—you went there to get potatoes, stock up on fresh wild mushrooms at a reasonable price, and buy greens; and the Tishinsky, which was the Moscow outlet for Smolensk and Belorussian produce, and the kingdom of the Antonovka apples.

I drove around the square in front of Belorussky Station, navigated the side streets that lead off Gorky Street, and pulled up to the Tishinsky. The crowd milling around the market gates was hungry to price out all that was available there—the potatoes, mushrooms, or cabbage—but the air was permeated with the scent of apples. It wafted over the market crowd and made nostrils flare at the thought of the crisp, sweet-and-sour pungency released like an explosion of life force at the first bite of an Antonovka.

I walked up and down the rows inside the green pavilions and under the plywood awnings erected outside. I took a close look at yellow-green, green-amber, amber-chartreuse, and golden apples, their cheeks swollen with juice. They were all Antonovkas. All these apples gave off the same unmistakable, intoxicating fragrance, like champagne. In the same way, all breast-fed babies, whether

1

white, black, or yellow, carry the sweet aroma of mother's milk. They are all babies. And all Antonovkas are Antonovkas—that's all there is to it!

But I was still looking, still trying to find the right ones. After searching all the rows, elbowing my way through the crowd and getting my fill of discussions about prices and varieties, I stopped in front of golden Antonovkas the size of tennis balls, gloriously fragrant with the scent of new cider and just beginning to develop a delicate rosy hue. I stuffed a whole bag full and lugged the apples to my car. In the square by the public garden, strewn with a mosaic of leaves, I found my battered and scratched Zhiguli, a veteran of Moscow traffic, and was opening the trunk when I heard a familiar cheerful voice.

"Hey! Long time no see! You never change, big guy!"

I turned around. Of course it was her, Lusya, from Apartment 33 in our wonderful old building on Pravda Street. I had moved out of the building five years earlier to the area of the River Terminal. Lusya, the wife of the restoration artist Vasya Ksyondzov, was still the same gorgeous leggy blond, except she seemed to have filled out a bit. "Statuesque," as her husband would put it. Lusya tossed aside her red backpack, from which bunches of parsley, chicken legs, scallions, and Lord knows what else stuck out, and threw herself at me with kisses.

"Lusya!"

"Hey, big guy!"

"What a surprise! You're the last person I expected to see."

"Where did you disappear to? You're a real Count of Monte Cristo!"

"Lusya, it's great to see you. Let me throw your bag in the back seat. Where can I take you?"

"What? Have you forgotten where home is?"

"Oh, I'm sorry, Lusya, I wasn't thinking straight. I just can't get over running into you like this."

I had reason to feel confused and to lose my head. In a single instant everything came rushing back at me, everything connected with the building where I had lived for thirty-four years, and from which I had fled because of one incident directly linked with Lusya.

We used to be great friends, Vasya Ksyondzov, Lusya, and I. After work I would stop in at the one-room apartment where I lived as a bachelor. It was really just a shabby hole-in-the-wall: half-clean, half-furnished, and never really livable. I went there to wash off the dust from the bronze and silver I used all day to plate vases, pitchers, and goblets intended as gifts. I would grab something quick to eat and dash over to the Ksyondzovs' place. I usually showed up later than their other friends, because the GUM department store, where I worked as an engraver, closed at nine o'clock. By the time I got home, cleaned myself up, and was ready to go back out, it was almost ten. Then I would go up to their apartment, settle into my favorite rocker in the corner under the date palm, and spend the entire evening listening to Vasya Ksyondzov's friends, all genuine artists who belonged to the Moscow Artists' Union, or at least to the Artist's Fund, argue furiously.

I never made it as an artist. I didn't have enough imagination, education, persistence, or even daring. I never got beyond sketching antique plaster busts with empty sheepish eyes and equally sheepish curls. The flowers I painted deserved to be put in the trash even before a vase or pitcher could be drawn in beneath them on the paper. And the people or animals in my pictures . . . never mind those incorporeal creatures! The only thing I was good at turned out to be calligraphy. Vasya Ksyondzov, a man both gentle and resolute, once told me this: "You know what, big guy, if you're born to be an artist, then to hell with it all, go hungry, live in poverty, suffer, go out of your mind. It will all work out in the end. One day you will be recognized. Fame and money will come to you at once. But you, you know I love you like a brother, and am sorry to have to say it, but you are a calligrapher. You should have been born before the first Russian printer, Ivan Fyodorov! And since that's the way it is, why should you suffer, tormenting yourself and waiting for the impossible, when you can and must have the good life tomorrow? You will never be famous, it's true, but you will make a good living."

And so I began to do inscriptions, engrave greetings, and transfer to glass, metal, or porcelain someone else's words, exotic scripts. In short, I became a good, honest craftsman. No, I didn't tear myself apart and didn't feel in any way inferior to the real artists. I had no complexes whatsoever. While the Ksyondzovs' crowd were arguing about their idols and pariahs, about realism versus surrealism, about their work and luring rich clients to their studios, I sat quietly in the shadow of the date palm, like a pilgrim who has walked under the blazing hot sun all day and reached an oasis. I sat there and listened to the evening babble, as pacifying as the eternal murmur of a brook.

The Ksyondzovs put little Seryozha to bed by nine o'clock. When I came in he was usually asleep, his light already out. I would kiss his chubby little nose. He didn't wake up, but he knew that I had been there all the same. In the morning there would be a clown dancing near his crib, or a camel slowly chewing a thistle. Or else a balloon blimp hovering near the ceiling. On Sundays I took him for a walk to the park in the Maryina Roshcha area to give the Ksyondzovs a little time off.

Occasionally just the three of us, Lusya, Vasya, and I, spent a quiet evening together. We would have some wine, a glass or two, just to whet the appetite, and eat sandwiches, which Lusya put together masterfully. Anchovies with grated cheese, roast beef with parsley and cucumber, hard-boiled eggs and lettuce, salmon with black currant chutney, and many others that I no longer remember. Then we'd have tea and just talk about life. I talked about routine things, about my department store. I warned Lusya when to come to the store and whom to see if a shipment of Western-made goods was expected. Lusya recounted the endless personal histories of her female colleagues at the editorial offices of Comet Publishers. Endlessly different and inconceivably identical: love, marriage, a baby, divorce, a self-absorbed lover, agony over the passing of the best years. Or: love, marriage, living with a man she no longer loved because by then there was a baby, and yet another unfaithful lover. It is a terrifying thing for a couple to rip apart the fabric of a marriage, moth-eaten though it might be by mutual reproaches and wrongs, and then stand there naked before the world. It is also terrifying to break up with a lover—will the next one be any better? All of Lusya's stories were full of passion, intrigue, and violent endings. The kind of thing you'd go to see in a movie.

Vasya would cheer us up with his glittering success stories. Everything always turned out for him. He restored a painting by an old master so well that it was immediately sought by the best museums. His work brought both acclaim and money. He played regularly with filmmaker Nikita Mikhalkov—a pool shark—and never failed to win. Foreigners brought him gifts of special Dutch brushes out of gratitude just for permission to observe how Vasya Ksyondzov cleaned gritty dust from the surface of an old painting undergoing restoration.

Once, however, Lusya changed the character of her stories. That is, the story of one coworker departed from the traditional pattern.

Not long before, Sashenka Brodsky had come to work at Comet Publishers. She was a grandniece of Brodsky, the famous painter who studied under Repin and later painted Lenin. A petite and demure woman of twenty-eight, Sashenka was an uncommon specialist in the assembly of photo collages from bits of drawings, watercolors, paintings, and so forth. And of course, at the next hen party (at Comet they had a lot of all-girl parties), it was Sashenka's turn to be accosted with questions of "What's it all about?"

"It's all about one thing," Sashenka sincerely and sadly professed. "I've been married three times, and now I'm alone again."

"Any children?" someone asked.

"I've never had any. But I haven't given up hope," Sashenka answered so simply and naturally that nobody bothered her with further questions.

At this point, Lusya obviously realized that she had said too much. It was too late, however—words are not sparrows. . . . Lusya shook her finger at me: "If you ever meet her, big guy, don't you give me away. This is precious information for a solitary tomcat like you."

"Lusya, what makes you think that I need your help with women? Didn't you ever notice there are hundreds of beautiful women at the store, on every floor? And if I were desperate, I could ask Vasya about artists' models. Right, Vasya?"

Vasya was watching a boxing match on television between the USSR and the USA and couldn't have cared less about Sashenka, her husbands, and her fertility problems.

"Uh-huh," he muttered, just to get rid of us.

But a story becomes a story, rather than a casual incident on a streetcar or a chance encounter in the subway, because it goes on twisting and turning without asking permission from its dramatis personae, while a chance encounter can be broken off and forgotten.

Sashenka began to frequent the Ksyondzovs' evening gatherings. Lusya, a kind and sociable person who liked to do nice things in that simple, ingenious Russian fashion, began to introduce Sashenka to Vasya's friends. There was a succession of three or four of them. The sculptor Abkin was a burly lover of fun and drink, with curly black hair; Sashenka spent about two months with him. Alik was a designer at the auto works, scrawny, sinewy, and silent; she went away with him for a vacation on Lake Seliger. Then there was Dr. Pekhov from the Artists' Fund Clinic, whom we all, of course, called "Dr. Chekhov"; Dr. Pekhov announced that he was going out of town on business, but what he really did was hide out at Sashenka's apartment for the whole week. And, finally, there was Kurt Schneider, a graphic artist from East Germany who came to Moscow to draw churches and immediately fell in love with Sashenka Brodsky. Things fell apart with him, too, despite the promise of a "fiery cocktail"—a mix of German and Jewish blood. Sashenka remained, as before, sweet, charming, and . . . childless.

One evening we somehow found ourselves a foursome: Lusya, Vasya, Sashenka, and I. That is, I dropped in on my friends as usual, and Sashenka, as she put it, "Couldn't bring myself to devour all those exquisite pastries from the Stoleshnikov bakery all by myself." In a cardboard box, flung wide open like a winged-dragon kite, lay little pink horns filled with whipped cream, chocolate potatoes, slices of pastry logs, pieces of sponge cake with rainbow frosting, and little baskets filled with cherries. We drank tea and chatted. Actually, it was the first time I really spent a whole evening so close to Sashenka, talking to her.

I usually sat in my rocker under the date palm, sipping my wine, listening to the tapes, and watching whoever was dancing. Sashenka was always in motion. Her form, slight like a hummingbird's, and her shining black hair, flying around her shoulders, seemed to be everywhere. Her current admirer, tightly pressed to her girlish body, whispered sweet, inviting secrets. I imagined to myself what they were whispering, but could not picture myself being in their place with Sashenka. I just felt too much a part of the Ksyondzovs' apartment, like the palm tree, the paintings, the rocking chair, the doors to the balcony. People could walk around me, push me aside without noticing me, and just pass on by.

And so there we sat, the four of us, drinking tea and eating pastries from the Stoleshnikov bakery. Lusya was dressed in some sort of impossibly wild outfit, half-kimono, half-evening gown, her magnificent breasts erupting right out of this "robe of Venus," as Vasya called it. Sashenka was wearing velvet leggings that accentuated her ingenue's figure, and a fluffy, pale-blue angora sweater. Vasya had pulled on a black Russian peasant shirt, "à la Gorky on Capri." I had shown up in white canvas bell-bottoms that I had bought for a few rubles from a drunken retired midshipman. Out of the blue, between the second and third cups of tea, Sashenka asked me casually if I knew anything about Indian lettering. She was working on a catalog for the Roerich exhibition. I said that I had once studied Indian scripts and had even done something with them, but that I had forgotten the order of the characters, and would need to refresh my memory. Sashenka persuaded me to do so. I located my sources. We started working together. Our relationship lasted a total of three months. Then I fled. I fled from Sashenka's gaze, which at first absorbed me with adoration and hope, and then, after one month, and another, and then a third, with puzzlement, disappointment, and finally, with vexation.

I fled. And yet things had never been so wonderful for me with anyone as they were with Sashenka. I ran off to a friend's house on the other side of Moscow. I never sent any news about myself to anyone at the old building, even the Ksyondzovs, although I missed them, little Seryozha in particular. I was ashamed for what I did, but also for Sashenka, for the Ksyondzovs, for the whole world. Later I got married. Kira and I were able to exchange our dingy studios for a two-bedroom in that high-rise building by the bridge over the Moscow-Volga Canal, near Khovrinsky Park. We had a little girl, Natasha, and I nearly forgot all about the whole business with Sashenka, although I did miss my dear friends.

And now, would you believe it, this unexpected meeting. Lusya and I got on the Leningradsky Prospekt, got off at the watch factory, and took a side street lined with poplars almost to the end of Pravda Street. But I didn't go all the way to the corner of our street, and pulled the car over across from a local pub.

"Do you want to come up?" Lusya asked.

"I can't right now. I'll come and see you some other time. I do want to see Seryozha and everything. Right now let's just sit together for a little while—how about this place across the street. You can tell me about Sashenka. How's she doing?"

"Everything's fine with Sashenka. Okay, let's go, just a quick drink, and I'll tell you."

We went in. It was early afternoon, around one o'clock, probably the only time you could get into this pub, which was popular with the young crowd. It was half-dark. Quiet jazz music. I ordered us both coffee and a little cognac. And this is what Lusya told me.

"For a whole year after your disappearance, Sashenka walked around like she was stunned or grief-stricken. No more affairs. A real Christ's bride. But all the time, as they say about artists who experience a creative slump, 'her soul was seething with potential.' Sashenka did an assiduous literature search. She started a correspondence with some British physicians experimenting with the implantation of eggs fertilized *in vitro*. She flew to Ulan-Ude to consult with experts on Tibetan medicine. All the current research was at her fingertips.

"There was an apple cider vinegar craze in Moscow. Everyone was making their own and taking it for all kinds of medical problems. So I suggested to Sashenka: 'Why don't you go buy some apples. You never know, it might even work.' I suggested it and immediately regretted it. Eve is the only woman who ever got pregnant after eating an apple, and even she had help from the Serpent, and from Adam, too. Besides, Sashenka was so depressed when it didn't work out between you two that she had no inclination to experiment with either snakes or Adam."

"When did all this happen?" I asked, taking a sip of cognac.

"Exactly a year ago. Some sort of weird coincidence!" Lusya continued. "Just like you and I both deciding to go shopping for Antonovka apples today, our Sashenka went off to market, to the

Leningradsky farmers' market, which is closest to her, and began to walk up and down the rows. She looked at some apples, turned a few over, took a whiff of some others, but just couldn't make up her mind which to buy—it was as though her whole fate depended on it. She finally spied some golden ones with the fragrance of champagne—smooth round Antonovkas. And above them was the smiling, golden face of a Korean farmer. His eyelids were puffy like ravioli. Under them flashed the narrow black slits of his eyes.

" 'Vely best Antonovka,' the Korean man praised his wares. 'And tseep, too!'

" 'And can I make good cider vinegar from your very best Antonovkas?' asked Sashenka.

" 'Yes, miss. Vely best Antonovka make vely best vinegal.'

" 'And will you give me the recipe for the very best apple cider vinegar from your very best Antonovkas? If you do, I'll buy your entire lot.'

" 'I terr you the lecipe and bling to your prace.'

"So they went to Sashenka's place. As you know, it takes at least two or three months to make good apple cider vinegar. And then you use it for a whole year. Business was brisk for the Korean, and he stayed in Moscow well into the fall. He murmured incantations over the jars, poured, strained, brewed, filtered, and finally announced: 'Cidel vinegal is leady, Sashenka!' And then he left."

Lusya finished her drink.

"Why don't you order me one more drink, big guy, for old times' sake."

I did. She paused for a while, then smiled.

"You still have some left."

"That's it for me. I have to drive."

"And go home to your wife," Lusya added. "Is she jealous?"

"Not particularly," I answered.

"And now let's drink to little Anton's health," she proposed.

"Little Anton? Do you mean Sashenka had a little boy?"

"A month ago. He's such a beautiful baby. Golden, like a ripe Antonovka. So, big guy, buy a present."

I took her back to our old building, from which I had once fled. And as it turned out, it was a good thing that I had left.

Translated by Maxim D. Shrayer and Victor Terras

Written in 1985 in Moscow and revised in 1994, "Apple Cider Vinegar" (Iablochnyi uksus) was first published in both Russian and English in the February 1995 issue of the short-lived bilingual magazine *Marina*. The revised Russian version, which the present translation follows, appeared on 9–10 November 1996 in *Novoe russkoe slovo,* America's oldest Russian daily newspaper.

RUSTY

In the salty longing for his wife (away on a three-month business trip), Lyampin bought a dog.

I've summed it up as "bought a dog," but the acquisition didn't happen all at once, although it was a result of the same longing, heavy and dense, that chased him from his apartment and kept him from working. Lyampin loved his wife and hated her business trips. He had hardly survived her last one—she had disappeared from home for more than two months, accompanying a delegation of mining engineers to Spitsbergen. Nobody knew Norwegian, and Irina translated the hosts' English into Russian.

Later, after her return, while they rolled together on the yellowish-white polar bear pelt, his face muffled in the rusty mane of Irina's hair, feeling that all of her was there with him, and forever (so he believed), Lyampin realized on what verge and above what precipice he had teetered without her. Only the set designer Noneshvili—Lyampin's friend and classmate from the Stroganov School of Art—had saved him. They had gone to Tbilisi, Georgia, where Lyampin tried to lose himself in parties and commissioned portraits, his pain and longing blunted. He had been finishing up the set for *The Hussar with a Guitar,* a new play being staged for the Russian Theater, when the telegram from his wife had arrived: "I am back home—Irina."

But this time—his wife was now off on another trip—he sank

to a new low. There were two or three sprees that began in the billiards room of the Moscow Writers' House and ended with him waking up in the middle of the night to drink Borzhomi mineral water and take aspirin and toss and turn in the bed. The sprees, rather than diluting his longing, sharpened Lyampin's endless malady; again and again he dredged up the circumstances of their family life, proving (to himself at least) that Irina was unhappy because of him, and was always ready to part from him, even for a business trip. They had no children. It was his—Lyampin's—fault. He didn't let himself reproach Irina—how could she, a sophomore at the university, have foreseen the abyss formed then for life, the abyss that still appeared in Lyampin's dreams as a cleft, covered with snow-white sheets (not snow but sheets)? Out of the abyss Irina's voice wafted, "I don't want . . . don't kill . . . leave him to us . . ."

᠔᠕᠔᠙

Having wasted two more days, Lyampin opened a book of business cards that he kept. Some time before, at the birthday party of the twin Rogunsky girls (who happened to be nieces of the famous general, the one whom Lyampin knew from having painted his portrait against the background of a tank), Lyampin had seen a longhaired dachshund. "Exactly Irina's color," Larisa, the twin's mother, said, nudging Lyampin with her bare shoulder. "And as loyal as Irina. She's going to have puppies soon. Oh, my little Rusty!" Wiggling her hips, Larisa slid into the kitchen to make tea.

Lyampin was finishing a slice of nut loaf when Rusty's owner—a strange, melancholy young woman—sat down next to him.

"I've heard you wanted a puppy?"

"Well, thanks," Lyampin hesitantly looked at his wife, who was lazily stroking the fibrous, copper-red fur that dangled from the dog's long ear.

"Perhaps we do want one. Right, Irina?"

His wife, sighing and smiling at the same time as no one but she could do, gazed at Lyampin indulgently.

"She looks so good next to your wife. And, besides, I'm especially interested in finding a good home for the puppies."

Lyampin, fascinated by the striking similarity of the color of Irina's hair to Rusty's fur (down to the smallest details), listened to the monotonous voice of the young woman—she was still trying to convince him—while examining his own fingers, rough from solvents, and the tender, long matte-white hands of Irina.

"Perhaps you're right," he said to Rusty's owner.

"Think about it and give me a call." Lyampin was given a card with the address, telephone number, and last name of his new acquaintance. Inscribed on it was "Member of the Committee for the Protection of Animals." And a picture of an owl.

The Lyampins didn't call about the dog.

Three years passed.

And now, missing Irina, Lyampin remembered Rusty. He woke up and found the telephone number of its owner. But what if there's already no trace of the puppies? Of course they can't be the same ones anymore. New ones were born. And could have been given away. As if this old maid were waiting for me! You wish!

Lyampin felt the longing again. He decided that it would be stupid to call. Spent the whole day wandering around the apartment, flipping through *The Master and Margarita*. It didn't console him. This time the famous novel seemed a hybrid of Gogol and Zoshchenko. Lyampin called himself a grumbler and a snob and took off for his studio. He hardly looked at one of his half-finished works; its boring contrivances and dull spots of color made him nauseous. He returned home. And once again he remembered Rusty.

As for Irina, he tried not to think about her; he needed her too much. He wouldn't allow himself to imagine her at that moment, somewhere in Tokyo, or Kyoto, or in God knows what Japanese city, connecting a group of engineers from the city of Krasnodar in southern Russia, frowning because of the language barrier, with their smiling, swarthy, lacquer-black-haired hosts. She impatiently tossed back her copper-red hair, the big swirling locks. No, no . . .

He forced himself to remember only Rusty. How she had sat on a chair between him, Lyampin, who was finishing his second slice of nut loaf, and Irina, relishing her coffee. He clearly heard the words of the owner of the longhaired dachshund: "She looks so good next to your wife."

Lyampin dialed the number that the owl held in its shaggy, knife-sharp claws. A quiet and reproachful voice answered the phone. He asked for Gayane—that's what it said on the card, Gayane Akatova. The reproachful voice belonged to Gayane herself, the young melancholy woman, Larisa Rogunsky's friend. Lyampin reminded her who he was: "You know—the hyperrealist painter who sent you that slide of Rusty's portrait I did from memory."

"I received the slide."

"And how is Rusty herself?"

"It's as if you knew when to call. But, unfortunately, I'm not prepared to talk . . . especially over the phone."

"I wanted to ask about the puppy."

"You've decided now? After three years?"

"But I've always wanted it," Lyampin lied, and felt the wave of Gayane's responding breath; through the wires and membranes he felt her sigh.

"This is so weird and unexpected. Especially now, when Rusty is . . ."

He heard her sob and, then, the forbidding dial tone.

Half an hour later, Lyampin parked his Niva near the gates of a small townhouse on Kachalov Street. Gayane led him from a parlor,

crowded with empty cages and bowls filled with milk and grass—
the walls of the parlor were decorated with circus posters—into a
room whose outer wall, shaped like a lantern, opened into a garden.
The lantern belonged to an owl who sullenly occupied a claw-
scratched perch made of the trunk of a young tree ("alder," said a
voice in Lyampin's head). Something was hanging from the perch,
at first indistinct, but then transforming itself into the remains of a
white mouse: the owl hadn't yet torn its head nor swallowed its
bowels, so the head and bowels both dangled like a pendulum in a
horror movie. Along the walls, water played in greens and yellows,
locked into the aquariums' cubical spaces. The air, as well as some
stiff grassy shrub enclosed in glass, belonged to the living rubber of
grass snakes and pythons—or perhaps they were adders. The signs of
sacrifices to voracious reptiles were also present in the terrariums.

"Don't be afraid; they've got enough food—mice, frogs, mos-
quito grubs. My wards are oblivious to people. I'm only worried
about her."

Right next to the door (how had he not noticed?!) Lyampin
saw a small, precise version of Rusty—the very same longhaired
dachshund who had once sat between him and Irina at the Rogunsky twins' party. There was the color that both beautiful creatures—
woman and dog—shared: copper-red, blazing.

"She can't even drink milk from a bowl yet. I have to give her
the bottle." Gayane picked up the puppy, pressed her to her breast
(eternal call of maternity!), and stuck a red rubber nipple, placed on
a milk bottle, into the sharp foxlike snout.

"Like a real baby bottle," Lyampin said to himself.

"My Rusty—this baby's mother—died in childbirth. I knew
that she couldn't make it, the old thing. But I pitied her. I thought:
Let her enjoy puppies one last time. And see? She died. I gave the
rest of them to friends, as gifts."

"Naturally, Gayane, you've left this puppy for yourself? How
could it be otherwise?" (Why did she invite me?)

"No, no! I can't. What I'm looking for—do you understand?—is a good home for her."

"But why don't you want to keep her?" Lyampin was completely bewildered until he followed Gayane's eyes; they were fixed on the monstrous pendulum hanging from the owl's beak.

"I can't leave Rusty alone for the whole day. I work. I've got to earn a living for them." Gayane gestured to the animals.

So began the first weeks of Lyampin's fatherhood. He brought the little rusty-red dachshund back to his apartment, in which not only the mode of life but also the very arrangement of furniture and symmetry of carpets, rugs, and mats had been under the predestination of Irina's will. For the first time in their fifteen years of marriage, everything was turned topsy-turvy. Rusty crawled wherever she wanted, and later ran wherever she felt like, leaving huge—for her size—puddles on the floor and pungent spots on carpets and rugs. Besides that, the little shaggy creature howled, yapped, and yelped so sadly next to the sofa where Lyampin tried to sleep that he, unable to bear it, put Rusty close by on the sofa, every now and then touching her wet little nose—was she breathing?—to make sure that he hadn't smothered her with his body, as sometimes happens with infants. He had reached such a point of perfection and progress that by some devious means (could he say that he had adopted a baby from the Foundlings' Home?!) he procured French-made disposable diapers that he learned to dress the puppy in (they looked like little overalls); otherwise he would have had to change the bed sheets every morning. Rusty grew up, gnawed armchairs and sleepers, barked at imaginary enemies, and ate and drank from a bowl.

Two months passed. Lyampin began to take Rusty out into the February snow. She listened to his whistlings and tender requests: "Where are you? Don't run away! Here! Home!" Dogs from the neighborhood flirted with the young dachshund, who looked like a sneaky fox. Female dog owners spoke to Lyampin with interest.

He felt happy. For the first time in his life he didn't long for Irina, though it was the end of the third month of her trip. No, of course it wasn't that: he loved his wife madly. Thousands of times he imagined her coming back, bursting into their apartment, burning him with the red-copper flame of her insatiable caresses. He imagined how she would put everything in order and restore the wonderful family life that he so cherished. He loved her madly, missed her, waited for her . . . but didn't long for her. He wasn't suffering; he didn't languish in loneliness.

Sometimes Gayane would call him. Once she stopped by. It seemed that she wouldn't mind taking Rusty back. But not for anything in the world would Lyampin part with his "little daughter." That's what he called Rusty.

A telegram came. He went to Sheremetyevo Airport to pick up Irina. The weather was bad and the plane couldn't land. It was storming. The wind burst through hangars, whistling variations of Wagner's raging music. While he was sitting in a night bar, sipping coffee with cognac, he caught himself thinking and worrying more about Rusty—alone in the apartment for more than twelve hours—than about Irina being thrown from one airport to another to make connecting flights.

⟨⟩

"Lyampin, you're so sweet, waiting for me like this. I bet you haven't slept all day. Take my stuff into the car." Irina kissed and hurried him, shaking her rust-tinted mane covered with drops of melted snow, the way an impatient horse hurries her rider. "Go faster! I've been dying to see you, my love."

They drove at full speed along the Leningradsky Prospekt, trying to catch up on everything. Irina cursed joyfully, remembering her landings and takeoffs on the airfields of endless Russia.

"All the hotels are crowded. No place—can you believe it?—even to shower. But you've waited for me, haven't you, Lyampin?

Or did you have fun? Come on, tell me the truth! Did Larisa come after you, the old slut? I'll find out anyway. You know I will. Oh, you, Lyampin, Lyampin. I wish we could stop the car and right here . . ."

He answered in the same half-joking manner, burning with happiness and impatience. But he didn't dare tell her about Rusty. He didn't know why. He chased away everything that could spoil his meeting with Irina.

In the morning Lyampin introduced Rusty to Irina.

"What a cute doggy. And she already knows how to tell you when she wants to go to the bathroom?" Irina said, and Lyampin realized that Irina herself didn't want to spoil their meeting with a discussion of this unexpected new flatmate. But Irina could hardly hide her irritation when the puppy, perching her chin on Irina's feet, yawned and turned over on her back, asking to have her belly tickled; it was just at such times as these, when, relaxed by playing, Rusty would make a puddle. Irina ran out of the room squeamishly, and Lyampin, at first not knowing the seriousness of the situation, acted like a clown in the circus whose partner has screwed something up. He pretended to be angry at Rusty, and she, thinking it was all fun—entertainment for Irina—barked furiously and tried to pull the rag from him.

Within a week or two Lyampin clearly realized that it was no joke for Irina, and thus, not for him either. The gnawed wooden shoes recently brought from Japan; the dropped and broken bottle of French perfume (Lyampin's present to celebrate Irina's return); the greasy brown blotches from Rusty's paws, a result of her joyful dash around the apartment after a walk (the spring was long and rainy)—all this created an atmosphere of tension and siege. It was like a visit from a provincial aunt who—dear to one member of the family but not to the rest who feel no blood ties to the guest—annoys them and disrupts their quiet, balanced life.

Soon Rusty herself understood that she wasn't liked by her

hostess. From a trusting, tender, loving little animal, she turned into a gloomy creature, preferring to huddle in the apartment's corners. Lyampin suspected that in his absence Irina not only yelled at Rusty but also smacked her. "You know, Irka, it seems that Rusty is afraid of you. You don't ever beat her by any chance, do you?" He said it and then burst into laughter, hoping by his buffoonery to smooth over a rough spot that threatened to turn his comment into a fight.

"Stop being ridiculous, Lyampin! Don't you understand? I cannot be near her. I cannot!"

Neither Lyampin nor Irina noticed that, while they were talking, Rusty had crawled very quietly from under the kitchen sofa and reached her hostess's feet. It's hard to say now what the puppy had in mind—to protect her owner from an angry wife or simply to try to figure out what was going on by watching their feet marching in place? Was it another quarrel or the final break-up? Perhaps poor Rusty was making a last attempt at moving Irina to pity, to prove to her that a dog was still a dog, and that she would show her, Irina, total loyalty and faithfulness. Probably it was something close to that. The dog cautiously licked the hostess's bare heel, and then licked once more a little bit higher, where the slender ankle ran into the long shin, covered with little golden hairs. "Oh, nasty dog!" Irina screamed and kicked Rusty's long foxy nose with her heel. The dog yelped from the unexpected pain and offense, and then bit the most sensitive area, the delicate transition of the foot into the rounded, tanned calf of the woman now hated and hateful forever. "Disgusting dog, disgusting! You're both nasty, disgusting creatures!" Irina wept, her face turned to the wall, and Lyampin dashed between kitchen and bathroom, wetting a towel, washing the blood from his wife's leg, dabbing the tiny, needlelike cuts with iodine.

There was nothing left for him to do but put the trembling, whining Rusty into a tote bag, rush out into the street, start the car, and return the dog to Gayane.

The same owl reigned in the room, torturing the small bodies of torn white mice. The rubber shapes of snakes coiled and uncoiled in the terrariums. "Well, very good. Nothing can threaten my Rusty now," Gayane said, kissing the dog between its sadly drooping copper-red ears. "Come by if you miss her, dear Lyampin."

From that day Lyampin and Irina's marriage went sour, although nothing seemed to prevent them from reestablishing their former solid and solicitous life, with its excursions to theaters and artists' clubs, its invitations to friends' homes or quiet evenings spent at their own place, reading or watching television. The emptiness of alienation now inhabited their home. Lyampin moved into his studio, its windows facing the Patriarch Ponds. But he didn't find peace there either. He couldn't work. Every half hour he ran out to the balcony to check: Had Gayane taken Rusty for a walk? But long walks from Kachalov Street to the Patriarch Ponds exhausted the dachshund, and Gayane herself let Lyampin know that the less Rusty saw of her former owner, the better it would be for everyone—for him, Lyampin, most of all. Once, toward the end of the summer, Gayane simply didn't allow Lyampin in; he waited for several hours at the back stairs until he saw Rusty running around the yard, merry, downy, and happy.

Lyampin then decided to sell his cooperative apartment and move to the country. By that time Irina had gone through the formalities of divorce, sending to him the same Larisa Rogunsky as an intermediary. Lyampin signed the papers without even reading them, ignoring Larisa's flirtations.

ᏇᎳᏇ

Several years have passed since that time. Lyampin lives in a village in a log cabin, which he rents from an old woman (she moved to the apartment of her son, a driver for the Arts Foundation, who lives in Moscow, in the Sviblovo district). Some kind of soul-gnawing passion seems to compel Lyampin to draw animals, often dogs, more often rust-colored ones, sometimes with strange heads in which one can discern features of his former wife, Irina. He receives few commissions and doesn't mind making some money by drawing posters announcing movies and parties at the local dance hall. Recently, he was hired to teach drawing in the village school.

He seldom appears in Moscow, but when he does, people take notice. He usually stops his Niva—a rather run-down SUV—in a little alley parallel to Tverskoy Boulevard, near Pushkin Square. From the car he leads a fox—on a leash and muzzle—and solemnly walks her around the Boulevard, Kachalov Street, then the Patriarch Ponds, gathering crowds of curious onlookers, chiefly boys, as he moves. When the fox yelps, he calms her, saying, "Be patient, Rusty, be patient."

Translated by Thomas Epstein and Maxim D. Shrayer

The Russian original of "Rusty" (Ryzhukha) was written in Moscow between 10 and 15 April 1985 and was published in the émigré review *Vremia i my* 98 (1987). The present translation originally appeared in the *Providence Sunday Journal Magazine* (22 October 1989).

THE LANSKOY ROAD

I'm walking through a park in winter. The snow, February's snow, is bluish from repeated thaws and frosts. The knot-eyes of the yellow birch trees are black. The path is icy, rutted, slippery.

Suddenly, like a beating heart, or an ax cracking through ice: tap-tap-tap. A woodpecker, almost as large as a small child, its black head topped by a red cardinal's miter, nods at me from a branch in a pine tree. He nods at me and taps with his large, strong chisel-like beak, gouging out a groove in the waves of the pine bark.

No doubt about it: it's he, *my* woodpecker, the one from my childhood in Leningrad; the one in the pine tree overlooking the pond that encircled the orphanage on the former grounds of Count Lanskoy's estate. The very same Lanskoy whom Natalya Niko-layevna had married six years after the fatal duel between her husband Pushkin and the Frenchman D'Antès. The same Lanskoy who had been a friend of D'Antès.

That's how intertwined it had all been. Once, long ago, this very woodpecker told me of the legend of Pushkin, Natalya Niko-layevna, and Count Lanskoy. In those days too he would be spraying bits of bark onto the snow or—in summer—the grass; a shiny, sharp-leafed grass that grew on the banks of the pond amid the rushes. Bits of bark and pulverized brick were strewn over all the courtyards of Leningrad. Although it was 1944 and the war with Germany was ending, our fathers were still in the army and our

23

mothers worked all day in the factories. We children spent that post-siege Leningrad summer around one of the ponds or in the park. Greedily we gobbled up any legend, story, or tale that told of sorcery, magic, or miracles. We were hungry and impressionable. Here's one of the legends the woodpecker told.

During the first spring of Natalya Nikolayevna's second marriage, late on the night of June 5, Pushkin appeared at Count Lanskoy's estate. He had come from far off, from the direction of Black River, where he had dueled D'Antès. Standing quietly at the water's edge, his boots and pants caked with clay and mud, he was eyeing the windows of the estate. Inside the house all was still. He took in the sight avidly, scanning the rooms in which his four children—Grisha, Misha, Sasha, and Natasha—slept. On the other side of the house—facing Udelny Park—was the count's bedroom. The white night's milky, pink-tinged light was reflected in the windows of his room. The count was sleeping. But in between the children's and the count's room was another window, inside which the flickering light of a candle was visible, its light muffled by the June night.

Pushkin called: "Natalya! Natashenka." The voice struck the pond's dark water and ricocheted to the other bank. "Natashenka!"

The window opened. A woman's form appeared in the black frame. Behind her back, wings—shadows from the burning candle—fluttered. Natalya Nikolayevna was listening. She stared into the sleepy garden and then at the silent, dark pond. She could hear Pushkin's voice, carried from somewhere beyond the pond: "Natalya! Natashenka!"

As she blew out the candle, she could discern a dark shadow rooted to a spot under the pine tree on the distant bank, near the road to Black River. She shivered, although the summer night was warm. It was the eve of Pushkin's birthday, and she was unable to sleep. She wrapped herself in the black cashmere shawl that Pushkin had given her the summer before the duel. She wrapped herself in the shawl and sat remembering words and deeds as she reread Pushkin's letters. She was the Countess Lanskoy now. And she did love her second husband. She was grateful to him for the patient devotion with which he had waited the six long years after Pushkin's death. She was grateful, too, for his having taken her children under his charge and for the adoration she had discerned in his eyes, even in that far-distant time when she had been considered D'Antès's *object* (Count Lanskoy, in order to have the chance of seeing Natalya more often, had taken to chasing after her friend Idalya).

No, no! It couldn't be . . . She hadn't heard any voice. She was suffering from hallucinations brought on by the magnetism of the white night. Everybody these days was taken with it: magnetism, spiritism, mesmerism.

"Natalya!" This time she heard the voice distinctly, unmistakably—it was that impatient, fervent, and beloved voice that pierced her soul; the voice she had never been able resist or ignore, even on those days when all she had wanted was to be left alone.

The black shadow stood near the pond's opposite shore. Only the night and water separated them. It was a man; a man of medium height, strong, spirited, and vigorous. He was untying a rowboat that was moored to the distant dock. The boat was normally used by a Finnish milkman who raised cattle only a mile down the road, in the direction of the Ozerki Ponds; and there was also a Dutch greengrocer who occasionally used it.

The rowboat skimmed easily over the black water, obedient to the strong arms of the oarsman. Both terrified and exultant, she recognized him, her Aleksandr; she knew him by the shape of his hands, the slope of his neck and the bared, insatiable teeth visible through the half-open mouth. It was he. Vivacious as ever. He was hatless, and wearing a rumpled frock coat; blades of sedge grass were entangled in his wiry, dark brown locks; his pants were stained with clay, and farther down, just below the boots, were still darker patches, stains from the dew and water that had spilled over the side of the boat.

Pushkin took Natalya Nikolayevna into his arms and guided her into the boat; only then, after carefully freeing his hands from her cashmere shawl, did he gently kiss her, on the nape of the neck.

"Give me your hand, Natashenka."

She offered him her left hand, because on the right one she wore Lanskoy's wedding ring. Pushkin slipped his own ring onto the ring finger of his beloved's left hand—a hand the color of water lilies. It was a signet ring with a black stone setting, engraved and inscribed with ancient, squiggly letters reminiscent of musical notes.

Pushkin spoke: "This stone possesses a special fluorescence that makes us invisible to others on this white night."

Rowing across the pond they reminisced about the past, recalling bygone years that had slipped away as diaphanously as the canopy of the northern night. They recalled fond moments with each of their children; their births, their baby prattle, their games and illnesses. Sometimes they would stop the boat in the middle of the pond, sometimes moor it at the far bank—there, where the shimmering, entwined branches of a willow tree overhung the pond like the gnarled fingers of a violinist. Finally, when the orange stripe of dawn began to rise about the Forestry Academy Park, he took her back home. Taking leave of him, Natalya would then return the signet ring to Pushkin until the following summer.

It continued this way for several years. Pushkin would appear at the estate on the eve of his birthday, spend the night in the company of Natalya Nikolayevna, and disappear just before dawn, not to be seen until the following year.

During one of their secret nighttime vigils, however, a wind suddenly began to blow from the Gulf of Finland, heralding a storm. Pushkin entreated Natalya Nikolayevna to cut their meeting short and return to shore.

"Just a tiny bit longer," she implored, as if already sensing something inexorable and deadly. Unable to master a fate that had rent their lives once before, she nearly began to cry: "Just a bit longer, please."

He began to row to the far shore, toward the old willow tree's cherished shelter. Bumping into the thick sedge, the rowboat squirted out a bit farther into the water before it jerked and came to a full stop. Because of the unexpectedness of the jolt, Natalya Nikolayevna lurched forward, pitching headlong into the boat.

"Aleksandr!" she shouted, reaching out for Pushkin so that he would catch her in his arms.

There was no one in the boat except for herself. As if prompted, she gazed at her left hand. The signet ring was no longer there. She hurriedly went over in mind what had just taken place. Somewhere near the middle of the pond a wave had nearly swamped the boat. Natalya Nikolayevna had barely been able to save herself from falling overboard by grabbing hold of the boat's side. Something sharp and hard had caught on the outer gunwale—but she forgot about it immediately, exhorting Pushkin toward shore. The hard object that had scraped against the planking had undoubtedly been the signet ring set with the black stone as it slid into the water.

Natalya Nikolayevna couldn't row. She made her way on foot up onto the bank and through the wet grass. Slipping and sliding over the swampy ground that surrounded the pond, she retraced the horseshoe back home. The count stood waiting for her on the steps of the house.

⟩⟩⟩

The woodpecker told me this story a long long time ago; either in the victory summer of 1945 or the legendary post-siege summer of 1944, during a terrible heat wave. We children often disappeared to go swimming at the former estate of Count Lanskoy, which was now an orphanage. We thought it especially exciting to swim over there, jump out of the water, and run right under the nose of the orphanage's guard. Dashing for the dock, we then dived into the water and made for our side of the pond.

This activity had satisfied me until I learned about the legend of the signet ring with the black stone setting. Now I felt that I had to find the ring at the bottom of the pond. I had to help bring Pushkin and Natalya Nikolayevna together again. I had to help them even if it could happen only once a year, at the beginning of June. Although I didn't understand it then, I can now see that I was trying to use the magical ring to bring together my mother and father, who had been separated by the war.

I had a friend at the orphanage by the name of Dimka. Together the two of us managed to steal a rowboat off which the orphanage guard used to fish for perch and crucian carp. Dimka circled the middle of the pond, keeping to an imaginary line connecting Natalya Nikolayevna's bedroom window to the thicket around the old willow tree. As Dimka circled, I dived and then dived again, each time dragging up from the pond bottom hard objects that to the touch felt like a ring with a stone setting. I began to get tired. Lying in the boat to rest, I could feel that I needed more time in order to still my heart—it was beating like a fish on a hook. Finally I dived again and, rooting around the bottom with my right hand, found something round and metallic. It had to be the ring! I pulled at it but it wouldn't come, as if it were attached to the bottom. Straining with my whole body I pulled again, and my feet got tangled up in some netting—the guard used nets for fishing. Although I was nearly out of breath I felt I had to keep trying, had to get the ring; otherwise I'd be a coward and traitor and would have to give up my dream of retrieving it. I tugged at the ring but only succeeded in getting more and more tangled in the net. At last I felt my strength giving out.

A force—which science would call buoyancy but in my opinion was the life force itself—carried me to the surface. Through a haze I can remember my friend trying to haul me back inside the boat. He was shouting something, tugging and yanking until he himself fell in. Screaming savagely, he began to flounder about under the water, not knowing whether to surface himself or to continue trying to save me. Two or three more times I floated semiconscious to the water's surface—semiconscious but conscious all the same, because even now I can remember clamping my mouth shut with one hand (I didn't want to swallow a single drop of water), while with the other I squeezed my fist, clutching at the ring. I grasped it so tightly that I was unable to take hold of the side of the boat. Everything went blank.

I opened my eyes. Above me I heard the sound of pine branches banging against each other. Dimka wasn't there beside me. Instead, a man with a sunburned face and large lips was trying to prop my head up as he massaged my chest. The stranger's curly hair was tangled, and sweat streamed from his brow, circling around the bushy sideburns that covered half his cheeks. At the sight of my open eyes the anxiety and sadness in his own penetrating, blue-gray eyes disappeared.

"Yes, little brother, let me just turn you over for a moment. I need to pour some of the water out from your amphora." The curly-haired man bared his teeth, smiling mischievously.

"I didn't swallow any water! I kept my mouth closed, and my fist too!" I shouted, remembering the ring.

My fist was empty. I saw a silver ring with a black stone setting on the little finger of the stranger's left hand.

"My dear, desperate brother," he said, "you will sink many times in your life, and many times you'll swim back to the surface; many times you'll touch bottom before returning to the wide world. Adieu, dear brother, live long and well."

The stranger brushed against me lightly, and then, giving a

shake to his curly head of hair, set off down the Lanskoy Road in the direction of Black River.

Translated by Thomas Epstein

This autobiographical tale adds a page to the rich mythology surrounding the life and oeuvre of Russia's greatest poet, Aleksandr Pushkin (1799–1837). Originally written in Moscow in 1985, "Lanskoy Road" (Lanskoe shosse) first appeared as a chapter in Shrayer-Petrov's memoir-novel *Druz'ia i teni* (Friends and Shadows) (New York: Liberty Publishing House, 1989). A revised Russian version, which Thomas Epstein follows in the present translation, was published in the Los Angeles weekly review *Panorama* (2–8 February 1994) and appears in English for the first time.

YOUNG JEWS AND TWO
GYMNASIUM GIRLS

A small boat was disappearing over the horizon. Judin walked on the shore, tracing the high-water mark in ridges of seaweed. His friend Eusebius, lost in thought, hadn't even heard him suggest they get something to eat. The pointed shadow of a wind-twisted cypress on the shore lay across the waves, lengthening in the setting sun.

All at once the two young men heard voices, and then footsteps. Two girls followed a thin path to the beach. They wore tunics hemmed with tricolor ribbons, the dress of the Gymnasium of the Arts, a large white marble building on the outskirts of the Scythian city-port, a Roman colony on the Black Sea. The two Scythian girls appeared to be cutting class, running off for a few hours of sunbathing.

As the girls came onto the beach, they began to run. Then one of the girls—the taller of the two, who had dark, luscious hair—pulled off her tunic with a single shrug and abandoned it on the sand. Dressed only in the briefest blue silk slip, she dropped into the sand, and spread her strong legs and arms in the still-bright sun. She did not see the young Jews, who were hidden behind a breakwater and could not help looking at her. Then the other girl, who was willowy, fair-skinned, and blond, took off her sandals and sat down as close as she could get to her friend, as if protecting herself from the cool sea breeze. She did not take off her clothes. It was clear that the first girl was the leader—the stronger, the more brazen of the two. The dark-haired girl put her strong arms around her girlfriend and pulled her girlfriend's face to her own breast, stroking her fine blond hair.

Then the blond girl unbuttoned her tunic. The young Jews saw the tanned arms of the dark-haired girl stray about the breasts of her friend and caress her yellow flesh and pink nipples with great delight and gentleness. For a moment, Judin and Eusebius lost sight of the faces of the girls, as the faces joined in passion. The two Jewish men could see only their shoulders and hips and their tossing hair, a blur of interlocking bodies. After a few moments, Eusebius could not stand to look any more and gazed out to the sea. But Judin couldn't look away, shaking with desire. He was riveted to a space between the stones that let him see without being seen.

The silk undergarments came off the bodies of the girls and lay in the sand like two orchids, blue and yellow. The girls caressed one another. They moved only to allow room for gentle fingers and greedy lips—from bosom to nipple to belly, belly to neck and hips, their fervent bodies linking somehow closer and closer. They devoured one another with kisses, only their fingers moving more intimately and with more hunger than their lips.

Eusebius suddenly tugged Judin's sleeve. He wanted to come out from behind the wall, to join the girls, to free them and himself from unbearable arousal. Both young Jews were near the point of forsaking the rules they had been taught, their customs and beliefs. All they thought of was the possibility of unbelievable delight. The girls broke their embrace for an instant, completely out of breath. But then they embraced again, and the flax hair of the slender blond covered the lap of her dark-haired friend, whose head found its way between the hips of her blond lover.

The young Jews could contain themselves no longer. They jumped over the wall like barbarian raiders and fell onto the girls without warning. The girls, themselves overcome with passion, welcomed the newcomers. The beach filled with moans, with cries and yelps of delight, of rapture. Then all four dove into the surf to wash the sediment of lovemaking off their young bodies . . .

Later, the girls broke out the bread, meat, and wine they had brought with them to the beach. They were Scythians, Scythian women who had been taught to share bread and their bodies with any man who looked on them with love. They had no inhibitions. Talking, lying in the sun, making love, it was all the same, all healthy, all good, all sweet. Before long they were talking about the Gymnasium, talking as if they had known these nice "Greeks" (for that was who they figured Judin and Eusebius to be) all their lives. Though they were together only briefly, two couples emerged: Eusebius and the dark-haired girl, Judin with the blond one. The four of them remained together as they ate, and during horseplay in the water. Before long, a new wave of sexual feeling overcame them, and they paired off again.

After a time, the girls signaled to one another, broke off, and went to the sea to swim and chat. They walked out until the water was waist-high. When they turned, the young Jews could not take their eyes off the girls' breasts, which lay amid their streaming hair like forbidden fruit partly hidden by leafy branches.

At last, the sun fell to the horizon, and the four joined for one last bite to eat. The girls were sorry to go, but they had to be back at the Gymnasium for the evening sacrifice, which took place in the Temple of Juno.

"Is it true, as people say, that the Romans decided to let foreigners return to their homelands? That the Greeks, Jews, and others are leaving?" asked the blond girl, after swallowing an oyster's briny flesh.

"That's what my father says. But they can only leave if they pay a ransom. My father, he knows everything. He says it's a good plan, that it will make the Empire rich. It's the Jews. All we want is for them to leave behind their money," added her girlfriend.

"I guess he's right, Veronica. If we shake those aliens really hard, there will be enough for hundreds of years of holidays."

"But you are forgetting about the Romans," said Judin. "It's for Rome. They're not going to let the Scythians keep a single denarius." He was thinking about the time he was treasurer of the student association, which had to pay a ten percent tax to Rome.

The blond girl, Illiria, became very agitated. She jumped to her feet, now wearing only her blue silk slip, and marched in place on the hot colored pebbles of the rocky part of the beach. She ran her fingers through her hair, and her hair heave like brushes of feather-grass under the steppe wind. Something about what Judin said made her anxious. This Greek had touched a nerve, had reminded her how much all the foreigners were disliked in the Scythian lands.

"We're not forgetting anything. You and the Romans, you foreigners, you're all the same. We want you out. You can all get lost, for all I care," said Illiria, her voice now sharp and heated.

"Stop it, Illiria," said Veronica, trying to cool things down. "Let's not talk politics. We've had a great time with the boys. And I don't care who they are—Romans, Greeks, Scythians, whatever. All that counts is having a good time. Haven't you had fun with this guy? Now cool it. They're Greeks. We all worship the same gods and goddesses."

"I guess you're right, Veronica," answered Illiria. "Just tell them to stop talking about our Scythian problems."

"But we're not discussing just *your* problems," said Eusebius. "My friend was saying that even in your own land you Scythians, not to mention the aliens—Greeks, Jews—suffer under the Roman boot."

"Hey, Veronica, what's your Greek fellow talking about? He's trying to put us—Scythians—on the same level as the filthy Jews.

Oh Jupiter, strike me dead! That's what I get for sleeping with a foreigner."

"When you held me like that, moaning and yelping with pleasure, you didn't call me foreigner," said Judin. He was angry, huffing and puffing. He caught Illiria's wrist with his hairy arm. "You weren't complaining then about my ears or my nose. You weren't asking me to sing hymns to your idols. You weren't thinking about Juno or even Venus a little while ago, but only about me. So you should know, slut, that the arms and legs that held you as you orgasmed, these are Jewish arms and legs."

"Jewish? Jews?" cried Illiria, turning and then dropping into the sand.

Upon hearing Judin's admission that he wasn't a Greek but a Jew, as Illiria collapsed into the sand, Veronica buried her face in her knees and started to cry, her rich long hair spreading over her shoulders. The young Jews watched her sob, watched as her whole body trembled.

"What have you done? Why did you tell us? Now she will report us both to the secret police! We'll be kicked out of the Gymnasium for sleeping with Jews. Our parents will lose their government jobs. We're ruined. Why did you have to tell us you're Jews? Oh Gods, save me," Veronica cried.

"You mean *that's* the problem? Not that we *are* Jews. Just that we *admitted* to being Jews? You don't hate us, you don't detest us for what we are?" said Eusebius. He turned to Veronica, his face ashen in color. Tears appeared in his eyes.

"Of course not. I knew who you were right away," said Veronica.

Eusebius took Veronica's arm and looked with new hope into her eyes. "But why does your girlfriend hate us so much?"

"I don't know, I really don't know. Please help me. Otherwise there'll be a trial, an investigation. And everyone (O gods!) will know we slept with Jews. The secret police will force my parents to plead guilty, will say it was because we have had bad blood, that it was my blood that pushed me to lechery with Jews."

"Bad blood? What do you mean, Veronica?" said Eusebius.

"Swear you won't tell?"

"I swear on the Star of David."

"My grandmother was Jewish. O gods, save me! Make a miracle! Forgive me!" A new wave of sobbing overcame Veronica, and she fell back in the sand.

Without another moment's hesitation, Eusebius stood up and dressed. Once dressed, his entire appearance changed. All the joking, the ease, the excitement were drained from him. Suddenly he seemed serious and mature.

"Stand up, Illiria," he said, touching the blond girl's arm. "And you, Veronica, dry your tears. Do you see that breakwater, that wall of stones over there?"

"Sure! But who gives a damn about a pile of rocks?" said Illiria slowly.

"I see the rocks from which all our bad luck came," added Veronica, looking up for the first time.

"You just look behind those rocks, and you'll discover who we really are. Our uniforms are hidden there. We're officers in the Imperial Coast Guard. Hurry up! We'll show you our bronze helmets and long spears," Eusebius said, turning to the two girls.

"Really? You were joking when you said you were Jews, weren't you? You see, Veronica, it *was* a joke. A joke. I couldn't have made a mistake like that. *We* couldn't have made a mistake like that, right?"

All at once, Eusebius saw two points of light on the horizon, two fishing boats.

"All right, girls, great to meet you. But you're going to have to leave the beach. See the boats coming in? Our ships are getting ready to land. We can't allow civilians on the beach. Sorry. Judin, please show the ladies the way back to town."

Then the girls got up, quickly dressed, kissed Eusebius good-bye, and left with Judin on the path that led from the beach to the city, walking briskly, as if they were following orders.

Translated by Michael Fine in collaboration with David Shrayer-Petrov

"Young Jews and Two Gymnasium Girls" (Molodye evrei i gimnazistki) was begun in Moscow in 1984 and subsequently revised twice, first in Pärnu, Estonia, and later in Providence, Rhode Island, where it was completed in 1989. The Russian original was featured in the Baltimore biweekly émigré magazine *Vestnik* (29 December 1992). The English translation appears here for the first time.

HE, SHE AND THE OTHERS

He was carried inside with a fractured skull, blood oozing through a hastily fastened handkerchief. She helped her husband into bed, unable to get an explanation of what had happened from the Other One—he who had carried her husband inside. Out on the street it was one of those black and icy nights at the height of winter. She helped her husband into the bed they had not shared for more than a month. She slept alone in the bedroom in their large Egyptian-made bed. He slept in his den under a wall adorned with a tapestry. In the bedroom remnants of their former, loving family life were still evident in the photographs of the children and the dresser of Karelian birch, with its marble inlay and various hidden drawers into which strangers could not gain entrance. Nor could the children—little Sasha and Masha. In contrast, everything in his den evoked the life he led outside the family, his summer world of geological field trips in search of uncatalogued rocks of various hues and patterns. Even the photographs inside the den had a dry, severe quality, nothing like the family shots. In one of them he sat astride a shaggy packhorse on a glacier somewhere in the Altai Mountains; in another he stood at the top of a rock formation that jutted out from a dry riverbed; in another he was with the participants of an expedition.

Forcing herself to master her resentment and rage, she returned to their bedroom. He lay motionless, occasionally moaning, his breath shallow and irregular. In a hurry to live.

In a hurry to live it up, she thought coldly, as if thinking about a stranger. She had caught herself in a blasphemous thought: she didn't feel sorry for him. But something had to be done anyway, although she didn't know what or how. Nor did she know why she was afraid of doing what was usually done in such cases: calling the paramedics. She couldn't bring herself to dial the number.

I should ask him, the thought recurred to her. She watched him, waiting for his eyes to open.

"I'm going to help you undress and change your bandage. You need a clean one," she said to her husband.

"You don't have to. I'll do it myself. Just make the bed in my den, please."

"What about the paramedics? I can call them. Or maybe a taxi—we'll take you to the emergency room, okay?"

"No, nothing. It will pass. It's nothing. A scratch."

"Well then, iodine at least. To prevent infection," she spoke dully. Equally dully she helped him to his couch and then—after a moment's hesitation: hadn't she only recently done it?—changed the bed linens.

The children slept soundly, resting up for tomorrow's day at grade school (Sasha) and kindergarten (Masha). Sasha, their son, was a perfectionist; he always received top grades at school and made sure to leave his satchel standing in the hallway next to a smaller, sateen bag in which he kept a change of shoes. Sasha took after his father. The daughter, Masha, didn't—she was absent-minded, messy, and something of a smart-aleck. Her dolls were scattered all over the apartment, like drunken guests. Masha took after her mother.

On the couch he grew quiet, having daubed his wound with iodine and replaced the handkerchief with a bandage. Next to the head of the bed he had placed a bottle of mineral water, Borzhomi. He always drank Borzhomi when he felt a fever or sickness coming on.

She lay on the bed but couldn't sleep, thinking that she shouldn't have refrained from calling the paramedics. It was all linked with her *story*. She didn't want a shred of their dirty laundry to be washed outside the house.

He couldn't sleep either, feeling the approaching fever, a throbbing in his legs and arms. Around the throbbing their story itself was wound, or rather a strand of it—a bright and terrible one, like a dream within a dream. An idiotic strand from that evening and the beginning of the night. And a confused and contradictory strand in which she had played a part. The part about her and the Other One, which she had told her husband about.

But she knew nothing of this most recent strand—the one that ended in blood. And yet she was certain that it was a result of (and punishment for) her association with the Other One.

But punishment for what?

ᗰᗰᗰᗰ

It had all begun with a phone call from her girlfriend. Even before her first date with the Other One, the girlfriend managed— through hints and allusions, a well-placed ellipsis or two—to instill confusion in her soul. For two days (her girlfriend wasn't able to come by any earlier, and she herself was tied down with the children, both of whom were sick) she walked around in a state of constant anxiety that was like having a tourniquet tied inside her. Sometimes her fear seemed to lurk in whispers behind the staircase or the banging of the entranceway doors. Her girlfriend finally came one afternoon when he was at the Mining Institute, busy with his graduate students' research. Busy, too, because winter was the time for selection and analysis of the minerals collected during their summer fieldwork. He was already a full professor, a rising star. Yet even with his professorship he hadn't been able to break through to the rank of Corresponding Member of the Academy of Sciences. Was it his Jewishness? Perhaps his passionate nature, his very inno-cence—which was not foolishness, but rather a childlike quality of his, a saving grace of character—prevented it? Notwithstanding his professional genius, he was the kind of person some considered a fool.

"You don't suspect anything?" her girlfriend asked in an omi-nous whisper.

"About what?" she answered, knowing about what.

"He's still hanging around with her, even though he promised you."

"So what? They're both scientists. They have professional inter-ests in common."

"Professional interests? If I didn't want to spare you—"

"—then don't spare me. I don't suspect him of anything. How could I? Doesn't he take all his students, both male and female, with him every summer for fieldwork?"

"Oh my God, you're so naive! It's the city here, with its illusory taboos, which simply don't exist in the wild, where everything is permitted. Don't you know why an urban romance is a hundred times more exciting?"

"Okay, fine, but let's look at the matter rationally. This woman you're talking about: she's also a translator. She's translating his book into Swedish. How many people know Swedish? What can he do?"

"Of course. It's none of my business anyway. But when you end up with nothing for your pains, just remember."

"So you think," and she turned to the thing that set the whole story in motion, pouring tea into fine little cups of Chinese porce-lain, which he had brought back from a field trip to Tibet. "So you think that there's got to be brutishness every time a man and woman are alone together? With 'illusory taboos,' as you put it."

"It depends on the man and the woman. You'll excuse me for saying it, but she's a beauty, and totally uninhibited. You yourself know what he's like. A lit match."

"A Swedish match," she joked, but then became thoughtful, unsure.

"Imagination is a dangerous thing. Do you know about love Swedish style?"

"What has that got to do with it? We're in Russia."

"And what if she is shaped like an actress? In the Swedish manner. What if she has imagination, is ready for love and everything else? Plus, there are special circumstances here. He's been known to bring her little presents, flowers and boxes of candy."

"Fine, fine, whatever you say. But what does that prove?"

"It proves everything. Don't you understand? Everything."

"So what you're saying is that, if they're alone, it's right into bed," she defended herself against her girlfriend's pressure. "And what about conscience? Responsibility to a wife and family? And he loves me, you know. We've always had that."

"And what about romance, blazing passion, the excitement of risk? You deny its attraction?"

"I don't know—it's never happened to me."

"Well, let's try an experiment. Put yourself in his place."

"You're crazy! Mad! Whom would we experiment on, anyway?"

"But of course you know about the Other One. He's been pining after you for two years now."

"Come on, that's totally platonic!" she objected, but once again feeling unsure.

"We'll test and see where Plato ends and the flesh begins." Her girlfriend had her trapped. "You'll see what it's like to be in your husband's shoes.

ᏬᎳᏫ

That part of the story she didn't tell him. She didn't want to drag her girlfriend into it. What was the point in telling him the rest? Because now he lay in bed in his den, trying to soothe his fever with cooling waters drawn from a curative spa.

"Do you need anything?" she called through the door.

"No thanks. I was just drifting off," he answered, giving her to understand that he didn't want to be disturbed.

"Maybe we should at least call the paramedics to take a look?"

"No, I'll be all right. I've been in worse straits."

She returned to her own bed and more memories of their entangled story.

ᏬᎳᏫ

Her girlfriend set up a date with the Other One at her apartment. Rather, she set up two or three meetings. That is if you count the second rendezvous when they went out to a restaurant for dinner, first meeting at the girlfriend's apartment. They went as a threesome—she, her girlfriend and the Other One—just in case they needed an alibi. The Other One might be out on a date with her girlfriend, and she was there as a third, their mutual guest.

The first meeting—half of which took place in the presence of her girlfriend—was taken up with reminiscences. The Other One spoke about his wife and his unhappiness in their joyless marriage, a marriage that had been sustained by concern for their daughter. Fortunately, their daughter was now standing on her own two feet, had been accepted to the Conservatory of Music and was even tutoring others. Their cares were over.

"And your wife?" she asked, trying to imagine just how the young colleague spoke to her husband during a secret date.

"What? My wife?" (in the same way her husband probably answered the question). "My wife is a very independent person. She heads a budget office. Earns more than I do. An actor's life is a humble one."

He worked at the Leningrad Malyi Drama Theater. An average actor, he usually obtained secondary, if respectable, roles as he patiently waited for the Distinction of Theatrical Merit (he'd get it either at the jubilee anniversary of the theater or on his own fortieth birthday). In contrast to her husband—an imposing, lively sort who caught fire at the slightest provocation—the Other One had the look of an even-tempered, handsome gentleman, with finely chiseled features and an elegant manner. He was a professional man of the world whom people liked to invite to parties. He had taken a liking to her long ago because she differed from his own wife by her even temper and gentle beauty. She and the Other One even looked alike—both had wavy blondish-brown hair that flew off into an invisible ether. Both had gray, frightened eyes and dimples—hers were on her cheeks, his on his chin.

Their third meeting . . . From their third meeting she fled in tears and shame. Out of shame and, more importantly, the awkwardness of it all, she began to bawl, telling her husband everything. She confessed everything in the hope of horrifying him by the shame and humiliation that he had inflicted on her by his relationship with his younger colleague. Of course she no longer doubted that he was having an affair with the young woman. What had begun as an experiment or test had completely overwhelmed her: she now understood the inevitability of the whole situation.

"What's wrong? Please, for God's sake, don't cry. What happened?" he asked, trying to find out what had happened, although equally afraid of what she might reveal.

She, in tears, in between teaspoons of valerian, amid hysterics and exits to the bathroom, told him what had happened during the third meeting.

ᏬᎳᏬ

She had met the Other One at a café on the corner of Lev Tolstoy Square and Bolshoy Prospekt. He was waiting for her at their agreed-upon table. They began to drink coffee flavored with her favorite liqueur—Benedictine. The room they sat in was empty because it was a typical slushy weekday evening, when people rushed straight home from work, trudging through icy gruel to subway stations and bus stops. On a night like this one doesn't want to be anywhere but at home. She herself had been only a stone's throw from Lev Tolstoy Square (she worked as an artist at the Lenfilm Studios). The Other One told her he had nearly managed to land a big part in Amirzanov's film, but at the last minute someone else had grabbed it. Suddenly he was told to go see the studio's director, who (he had been prepped by the actor who had stolen the part) asked for a written authorization from his theater permitting him to work at two places at once. When he went off to get it, the part floated away. She felt guilty in the presence of this good impractical man for whom everything was going wrong, at work and even with his wife.

"If not for you I might have shot myself," he joked, for the first time using *ty*, the familiar Russian form of "you."

"Don't despair, please you mustn't. It will all pass," the words broke loose from her.

"You think I shouldn't lose hope? That's what you think?" and again he breathed the familiar "ty"—a "you" that was like hands opening wide, hands from which she didn't recoil.

"I have no doubt. With your talent . . ."

They left behind a bunch of anemones on the cold marble table.

They hurried, having decided to go visit the girlfriend to see what she thought he should do about the stolen film part. Like him, she feigned an urgent need to see her girlfriend, knowing full well that the girlfriend would probably be at the clinic until ten o'clock, while her daughter (a twelve-year-old) would be at a rehearsal of her theater group. She would return at about the same time as her mother. Knowing all that, she nevertheless continued the charade of projecting what usually happens in such circumstances. What would he—the father of her children—have done? Carrying the key in her leather purse, she was excited in just the way that a girl is excited by the birth-control pills she takes without her parents' knowledge. They entered the apartment. She put on the music while he removed the bottle of leftover Benedictine from his coat pocket. They began to dance and drink the liqueur. The timid winter light edged past the flowers on the curtain tulle. She told herself repeatedly: Nothing is happening, we're just dancing, we're just drinking my favorite Benedictine. They sat on the ottoman and continued their discussion of how to get his part back.

"Aren't you hot?" he asked.

"A little bit," she answered.

"I'm half cold and half hot. I love you," came from his lips, as if it were a memorized line.

"Thanks," she couldn't find any sensible words with which to answer. "But we mustn't kiss, okay?"

"What do you mean we mustn't? I love you. We must kiss."

"I beg you, please don't force it."

But he wasn't listening, having skillfully removed her jacket and bared her thighs, which were wrapped in mouse-colored, woolen tights.

"I can see you're hot."

"Calm down, please. Get hold of yourself." How would it end? She felt herself stretched over a chasm between curiosity and desire.

"I'll calm down if you'll promise to be natural with me."

"I'm being perfectly natural."

"What about the tights then? You said you were hot."

"I'll take them off, but you promise?"

"Of course, of course."

Removing the tights, she was left with her skirt and a man's plaid shirt of Japanese silk, which she wore under a short jacket.

"I love you and can't go on this way any longer," he began with another wave of passion, imploring her with his hands and kisses. Pulling away from him, she appealed to his good sense, repeatedly invoking the names of her children and husband, his own daughter. The Other One heard nothing, thinking only of lovemaking. She bought him off, insisting that they leave the apartment.

Suddenly he ran to the window and thrust it open. He leaned out and repeated several times, "I love you so much, I must have you! If I can't I'd rather hurl myself from this fifth-floor window."

She implored him to close the window, and nearly yielded to him.

At the point of no return the door opened and a girl entered— her friend's daughter. It turned out that the rehearsal had been canceled.

⟨ᴏᴡᴏ⟩

She returned home uncharacteristically bitter, cursing the boorish taxi driver, who invited her out for a cup of coffee and pizza. Her husband, going over some papers in his den, tore himself away from them just long enough to offer her a kiss. She wrenched herself from his embrace and, without taking off her Arctic fox coat and fluffy fur hat, scurried away, locking herself in the bathroom.

"What's wrong, sweetheart? Tell me! Something happen at work?" He scratched at the locked door. She wouldn't let him in and sobbed uncontrollably, as if she were at a funeral.

He went back into his den, losing himself in his work just as strong-willed, independent men can—men who have no knowledge of their own culpability.

Embittered and disheveled, she entered his den, holding between her middle and index fingers a small object that shone between her lacquered fingernails like a stream between rocks.

"You asked me what was wrong. I'll tell you. But first you tell me, what's this?"

"I've no idea what it is," he said, taking the earring of translucent stone from her hand. "That is, I see that it's an earring, but I don't know from where."

"Then please tell me, how did it end up in your jacket? I was bringing it to the cleaners—"

"—oh yes, now I remember. I found it somewhere in the street. I was walking, I found it, and here it is. But you, you silly—"

"—don't touch me! You're a loathsome creature. Loathsome in your betrayal and doubly loathsome in your lie! A disgusting coward, that's what you are."

"Please, calm down. I swear, I found it, it was simply by accident."

"And her, that other woman, was she by accident too? You sleep with her, you . . ." (here she let out a stream of obscenities). "You and she—"

"—now stop it," he cut her off. "There's a limit to everything. I'm not going to sit here and take this crap."

"Crap? Yes, dirt and filth: a dog's lust, that's your masculine nature. You're all the same."

Crying in bitterness and despair, she told him everything that had happened between her and the Other One.

He dressed and went out into a blizzard. He wandered through the city's streets, finally stopping outside the big mosque. Its dome was azure. And next to the dome rose the minaret's divine harmony. Once he and she had stood in such harmony. Once it had been just he and she. Now it had been befouled by the Other One. There was no way out.

ඥාශ

"There's no other way out. That's why I summoned you," he repeated to the Other One. After the vodka and beer they had consumed, his rage had subsided: all he wanted to know now was how it could have happened.

"I understand. I won't even ask for your forgiveness. There's no other way. You were right to call me out."

The Other One was referring to the phone call he had received right after the evening's performance. Now they were aimlessly walking amid the indistinct lights and muffled rustling of the few cars that continued to skid over the snow-covered streets. They happened upon two or three establishments that offered them temporary refuge. Gradually, as they drank, they approached the issue. For him, it was to demand honesty from the Other One, hoping against hope to obtain some unlikely but longed-for evidence of his wife's innocence. For the Other One: to defuse the situation, reducing it to a case of trivial male lust, which there was nothing—at least nothing on her part—to feel guilty about. At last, slipping the doorman ten rubles, they entered a dark and dirty restaurant located at the end of Kirovsky Prospekt, near a small stream that flowed with black, brackish water. Through the windows of the establishment they could see its unfrozen black surface, from which steam dully rose. Once more they drank vodka chased with beer, picking with their forks at potato salad.

"There's no other way out, you understand. I've been forced to resort to extreme measures."

"Of course, especially since I've been unable to convince you that there's another way."

"Good. It's decided. I challenge you."

"Fine, but where?"

"I've thought it all out. I've spent the whole evening at it. Let's go."

"Do what you think you must, since it's all my fault."

"I don't think you've understood me. I'm not going to do anything to you."

"Then what? . . ." the other vacillated in the restaurant entranceway, eyeing the passing taxicabs.

"We both will. First one and then the other. Is it still unclear? A fight to the death."

Plodding along and above the narrow banks of the turbid stream, they nearly found themselves embracing. The middle of the stream remained unfrozen, churning with hot, decaying matter.

"There's a stone. Let's draw lots to see who'll give the first blow on the head."

The rock was sharp-edged, as is usually the case with stones used for revetment.

"Let's do it the traditional way, with matches. You draw."

"I've got the one with the head." The Other One showed it.

"Strike away," he handed him the stone.

The blow fell across skull and temple. The Other One, shocked that he had been able to knock his opponent right off his feet, stood motionless, the rock in hand.

"Now it's my turn." Wheezing, he pulled himself up onto his elbows.

"Give it your best, if it's good enough," the Other One offered his head, going down on all fours for convenience.

He raised the stone and smashed it across the other's ear before himself collapsing. He began to vomit. The Other One applied his handkerchief to his rival's head and then dashed for a taxi. He dragged him up the bank of the black stream and into the waiting taxi. With persuasion and superhuman patience he was finally able to get the enfeebled man into his apartment.

৩৩৩৩

During the night, delirium set in. His temperature rose to 104°F. When he could no longer hold out against unconsciousness, she called the paramedics.

Three days later he died. The doctor patiently explained to her that his penetrating wound had been complicated by a rapidly spreading infection of the brain.

Translated by Thomas Epstein

"He, She and the Others" (On, Ona i drugie) was written in Providence, Rhode Island, on 16–17 January 1988, during the author's first winter in America. A lover of Russian literature will recognize gleams of a Pushkinian biographical subtext. The original was published in the Baltimore biweekly émigré magazine *Vestnik* (24 March 1992). The English translation is published here for the first time.

JONAH AND SARAH

for Maxim

Underneath the mosaic vault of a pine forest a tomtit whistles a silver trill: "Ti-ti-ti-ti-ti-tlitititlitli." Then he stops. The sounds stream along tree branches, droop down rustling trunks to the ground, fly away through blue vistas of sky. And again: "Ti-ti-ti-ti-tli-titititli."

Jonah woke up and listened to the tomtit; he wondered whether specks of the tomtit's music might be hiding in hollows, under hummocks, in caves—between roots of a fallen pine. The third or the very last "ti," say, would break off from the melody and hide away, never again to leave this heavenly forest. Jonah still put off the moment of final awakening, rolling from side to side, stretching, shutting his eyes. His dream just wouldn't come back. It meant that he had to get up and say good-bye to the pine forest. To go on looking for singing wood.

Yesterday he had bumped into a hazel bush. When the wind from the sea hit the bush, Jonah heard a song emerging from the thicket, so he started to work his tousled head through the leaves and branches, turning around, listening closer until he found the hidden singing branch. Noise from the seaside highway made his job harder: heavy trucks snorted, buses tore jets of air apart, cars hissed by like tracer bullets. Actually, people no longer remembered the sound of tracer bullets. Cars hissed by like fireworks. Jonah knew right away that he had drawn his lucky number. One more hazel recorder! He cut off the branch, shaved off the bark, and put the instrument-to-be into his knapsack. There were about twelve of them already: recorders, whistles, fifes, flutes, and half-finished instruments. This hazel branch promised to be the queen of his orchestra. Oh, if it could only learn the tomtit's song: "Ti-ti-ti-ti-tlitititiitli." He would then find musicians. And a soprano. But first he would create an orchestra. And each instrument from the moment of its inception would be exposed to music of Jonah's composition. He would have an orchestra of singing wood. This is all so hard to explain. But it is even more difficult to persuade someone that everything in the Universe is interconnected. Jonah has grown tired of explaining and persuading. He believed in the predestined meaning of the triangle: creator—music—singing wood. Thus far he hadn't once been mistaken.

For many years now—he stopped keeping track—he'd been wandering about the forests of the Great Expanse. It all started when he was denied permission. From a famous composer, a favorite of the public, a laureate, he was turned into an outcast deprived of everything. He was permitted only to have a roof over his head. And to give music lessons. And nothing more. They even confiscated his instruments: grand piano, cembalo, violin, cello, French horn, kettledrum—there are so many of them in a big orchestra! He used to treat those instruments like his family. And now he was alone in his studio face-to-face with the empty spots his instruments once occupied. It had suddenly turned out that the instruments belonged to the people. And Jonah had separated himself from the people of the Great Expanse. He was stripped of everything: no concerts, no editions of his music, no instruments, no musicians. And not a single one of the many female singers once crowding his studio would now dare sing Jonah's songs. Quite a turn of fate!

The forests of the Great Expanse were all that was left to him.

They say that composing music is kindred to mathematics. And mathematics is a child of logic. Jonah intuited that some day members of a new orchestra would be there to play his wooden instruments. Where would they come from? Who would they be? Outcasts, refuseniks like himself? Or some new folks? He didn't know any of this. But he had an inkling about something that would later pulsate and sing in his knapsack. Live sounds, the gifts of the forest. Music. Serenity. Warmth during cold weather—forests of the Great Expanse provided him with everything. And why would they otherwise call it "Great"? The first year after he had abandoned his life in the city, Jonah headed north—an old habit. How wonderful it felt there! He spent the whole summer rambling between Törva and Pärnu. A fishing reel jingled in his knapsack. A silver rod jutted out like an antenna. He fished for perch and roach. And at night he laid his thick head of red wavy hair between hummocks; his head itself resembled a big hummock, overgrown with fiery creeping grass. Yesterday, before plunking himself down under a bush like every night before, Jonah had cut off a hazel branch and stuck it in his knapsack.

Jonah finally woke up. Prongs of sun barely touched the clearing, as if the Almighty hadn't yet started his morning chores. Jonah urinated behind a bush. He then splashed some spring water over his face and hands. He walked around the spot where he had spent the night. Feeble bilberry plants with hard bright-green leaves looked like scales of ancient reptiles that had lost their way and frozen in time. Who had ever seen scales of ancient reptiles? One thing metamorphoses into another. Things make their way through the Great Expanse, even though it is fenced off from the rest of the world . . .

淙

At first Jonah headed northward, to Estland. To the same area where he now roamed. Back then, eight years ago in October, autumn caught him in northern forests. Trees and bushes became silent. There was nothing for him to probe in the deaf-mute forest. And nothing to risk. Jonah turned south. Thank God, the Great Expanse permitted such travels. He found an area in Colchis where one could get by even during the coldest, rainiest, chilliest weeks of December and January. It didn't take much to find food in the rich mountainous woods. Jonah baked chestnuts, caught trout, shot quail and black grouse with a bow. Herdsmen didn't drive him away. Georgian yogurt, *matsoni,* and goat cheese in exchange for his music and stories. Jonah advanced back north with the coming of spring. He would fall a bit behind, letting the spring take charge. He knew spring would grow his daily bread and push the green blood of trees. Jonah went after warm weather and food, moving closer and closer to Moscow. Once a year he would turn up in his place in the city. He paid the bills. He removed last year's leaves off his parents' graves and planted new flowers. Different guests stayed at his apartment. He recognized some of them and didn't recognize others. Wife. Daughter. Guests. His daughter would say, "Hey! That's you? (You're still alive?)" "I'm just here for the day. Good to see you all." He was glad to see them. Just as he was glad to see a waterfall at Plastunka. Once a year—a waterfall at Plastunka near Sochi. Where the river falls into Pontus Euxinus, the Black Sea of Jason and Medea. Once a year a monastery in Staryi Krym. Crimean cherry blossoms. A cherry mouthpiece for a flute. Polesie in Belorussia. Tula Zaseki, the ancient oak woods. And Moscow again. Just once a year his wife's curiosity, his daughter's shimmering "hello." She's grown up. Twelve. And now twenty. "Hey! That's you?" Papa. Father. Nick (Jonah-JoNick-Nick). It had all died off, shriveled up like foliage. He would change into his city clothes and go to the bank. He withdrew the money he had been paid for reprints and performances of his old songs and orchestrations and arrangements of folk music. And God knows for what else! They wouldn't let you die in the Great Expanse. (Remember, you are getting a small part of the whole you have destroyed!) By the end of the day Jonah usually had had enough. And he took off. His instruments knocked against one another, jingling and fidgeting in his knapsack. They reminded Jonah that there weren't enough of them yet in his orchestra. They summoned him to continue searching for other singing branches. He went north to the Baltic, to Estland, where he would roam around until October. Just like now, when it's early August.

In this heavenly pine forest all the joys of late summer have come together: multicolored meaty mushrooms; dark-lilac bilberries; scarlet lingonberries oozing pleasure; raspberries shaped like nipples. Oh, Lord! Everything is here to provide for Jonah, to excite him and cheer him up, to give him hope. Only a woman is missing in his life. It had happened a few times during the eight years of his wanderings. Even celestial rain pours not only into rivers, but also into repugnant hatches of sewers. It had happened. A soldier's widow in a boarding house on the outskirts of Rostov. Something smelling pungently of a crop barn, of dandelion juice, something sweaty, drawing Jonah into its fathoms. Like a swamp. Or another time, at the beach, at night, inside an abandoned bus near Koktebel in the Crimea. A homeless woman mumbled words of tenderness in a Turkic dialect. Little ampullas crunched under Jonah's boots. The woman's bare leg hung down from a torn bus seat. He left before dawn . . .

These northern berries inflamed his desire for a woman. A woman with a real face. Hair. Slender motions of her back. Angles and curves. A woman endowed with human speech. Whatever you say, his fifes, flutes, and whistles possessed a different sort of language—eternal, beautiful, universal. But none of them could say to him: "Darling." None could lean back, succumbing to the devilish fire of his red mane. "Darling. Come here." Not a single branch. Nor his finished instruments. That was his shortcoming, a potential failure of his entire project. It was like a creek that, if dammed, makes the sea shallow . . .

As a rule, Jonah avoided cities. He never traveled by car or bus. But this morning, now turning toward noon, he decided otherwise. What happened was that while walking around a clearing and eating berries, Jonah noticed a baby badger. The little creature was sleeping under a bush, snoring gently; his little paws, covered with dark-brown glossy fur, were sprawled out. Jonah put the sleeping badger into his knapsack. In the past Jonah had sold rare animals to pet stores. He needed money to continue his long journey. And there was a baby badger coming right into Jonah's hands. He wanted to take him to the store right away, get the money, and return to the forest. This season, he hoped to find two or three more branches for his would-be instruments. Soon, very soon now, he would have a full set of his own instruments made of wood. And then . . . Jonah tried not to think beyond "then." Deep inside we all know that *then* will be the end of all our quests and ordeals. But until then we brood, bustle around, mix and mesh with other human beings, oust each other. And then . . . Jonah wasn't thinking of the distant future. To create an orchestra capable of performing his music—that was his Promised Land. That was the purpose of his travels around the forests of the Great Expanse.

Jonah came to the highway leading to Pärnu. The highway sliced the pine forest in two. The sun was moving toward the section of the forest that opened onto the seacoast. A roadside ditch was overgrown with reeds. Between the forest and the ditch there remained a strip of land strewn with little wiry plants of St. John's wort. Some of the inflorescences had turned brown and withered. Others shot yellow stars above amber frog legs of leaves. Jonah sat down on the hot ridge of the ditch. He didn't feel like hitchhiking. He knew that sooner or later a car or a half-empty bus would stop for him. Around the bend there would have to be a stop for buses going to Pärnu. Yet from where he was sitting Jonah could see neither a shed nor a bench. Slowing down, a black Volga passed by. Jonah heard the brakes squeak. And the screaming voices. He picked up his knapsack and headed toward the bus stop. Two burly guys were dragging a woman out of the back seat. She was kicking, fighting, trying to hold on—with her bare legs—first to the seat, then to the door, then the legs of the guy's trousers—so they wouldn't leave her behind.

"Why don't you go fuck yourself, Sarah, you bitch!" one of the thugs shouted when they finally succeeded in dragging the woman out and dropped her, like a heavy sack, about fifteen feet away from the car. "Get some fresh air. Maybe you'll figure out how goddamn sick we are of you!" added the other one, shutting the door of the Volga. The car dashed off.

Jonah recognized Sarah right away. He thought he had abandoned everything, uprooted all connections. And now it turned out: not everything, not all. The woman wept, tossing in the grass and biting stems, howling and wailing, because she had been abandoned, and even the exhaust fumes of the car had dispersed in the forest air. How could he not recognize her! Eight years it had been, but those chocolaty legs, bared all the way up to the buttocks, were still as beautiful and alluring as during their last autumn together. Their first and last autumn. Before he was denied permission and became a refusenik. And before he left the city and the family. Before he left Sarah.

"They're gone. They're gone anyway. Don't cry, Sarah," Jonah touched her gently.

She didn't recognize his voice. And even if she did, she still thought she was hallucinating. Don't we sometimes hear voices of those who left us, those we once loved? And we don't just leap out of our beds and go looking for them in the corners. Sarah did not speak, still sobbing and yelping like a banished, beaten dog.

"They are gone. And I've found you, Sarah. Found again, like in Gagry. On the Black Sea, remember?" Jonah insisted.

She turned her face to him, lifting her eyes. The flap of her sundress hiked up, revealing her hips. Up to the black strip of her bikini. Shapes of grass-strings, leaves, and flowers were incised on her tear-swollen face like shells on the beach at low tide. Some of them even stuck to her cheeks and forehead.

"Jonah?" she breathed out. And she laughed and cried with joy. "Jonah, Jonick, alive! Am I dreaming?" Sarah kept repeating, overflowing with tears, blowing her nose, and cleansing her face with more tears of joy.

"Who were those guys?" Jonah asked. "Did they hurt you?"

"Oh, that's nothing, really, just a silly scene! I was the one who started the fight. In any case, just forget about them. I'm so happy. Everyone thought you were . . ."

"I don't really care."

"Of course. I'm sorry, Jonah."

"Listen, Sarah, don't talk to me like I'm insane. Although actually . . ."

"Do you mean to say that we both look insane?"

"It's the same to me. I don't care what one looks like. I've stopped judging by old standards."

"Me too. And those," she pointed in the direction where the Volga had disappeared, "those boys just like to make scenes. Now they're probably mutilating each other somewhere nearby."

"Why are you telling me this?"

"So that you'd understand why they threw me out."

"I don't care about it. At all."

"They threw me out just to fight for me."

"Shall I get you a cab?"

"I didn't want to choose either one. I just couldn't. And see, they're embarrassed to fight in my presence. Like children."

"Hey, boss!" Jonah shouted to the taxi driver. "The lady is going to Pärnu!"

Sarah stared at Jonah as if she was now only beginning to understand the meaning of his remarks.

"You want to get rid of me again?"

"Boss, you'll take her to town. Here's the money," Jonah pushed Sarah onto the back seat and gave the driver a twenty.

ᏽ

The stupid adventure on the highway disrupted the harmony of Jonah's day. First, an influx of memories. Jonah left Sarah about eight years ago, or so he recalled, without even writing a good-bye note. She had been alluding to something unforeseen. Ah, what! Who would have chosen to rummage through the premonitions of a little third-rate singer who hadn't even been the first to perform Jonah's new songs. Although she did try hard. She was willing to do anything. Anything! How vapid this sounded in those days when any singer, even the most famous ones, "would do anything" to get herself closer to Jonah. But Sarah did have something. He can remember it now. This morning, when he felt the soft touch of sunlight on the moss, the little badger's fur, and the berries, Sarah came to his mind. Yes, yes! Eight years ago he simply ran away from her after he had gotten it into his head that the whole world had rejected him. Actually, the disquieting and sentimental recollections of his eight-year-old love affair were now augmented by notes of vexation. Vexing anxiety. Now, instead of being in Pärnu in half an hour, he would have to walk to town. The same disquieting and sentimental pangs of conscience and self-protection that had earlier prompted him to give the taxi driver his last twenty . . . And now he would have to get there on foot.

The black Volga belonging to Sarah's young companions was parked on a narrow roadside. Jonah walked past the car. Ahead of him, on the beach, a stereo made piggish noises. The two guys were cooling off in the water after a senseless, brutal fight. Maybe it was the fight, the fight rather than the woman, that meant everything to them. Sarah merely half-opened their eyes to the truth. The guys swam and sang obnoxious songs to the accompaniment of a stereo, forgetting all about Sarah, their Volga and their night restaurant gig. Their upcoming gig.

Jonah had put a hunk of bread in his knapsack. Now he remembered about water. The baby badger was thirsty. Jonah was thirsty too. They both drank from a plastic flask. After they had both drunk their fill, and it was time for the badger to go back to the sack, Jonah noticed a curious expression run across the badger's furry face. Like a little smile. Or a tiny note of regret. And then the recorder that Jonah had carved last year found itself in the little animal's mouth. Actually the little badger wasn't that small; the sizes of the ashwood recorder and his mouth weren't incomparable. In fact, the ashwood recorder fit the badger's mouth nicely. After a drink of water, followed by a series of manipulations with the recorder, the little badger climbed out of the knapsack and stood on a path, tramped out in roadside grass. He now walked next to Jonah. In his right paw the animal held the whistling and singing recorder while he pressed his left one to Jonah's, palm to palm. Not only the sizes of the recorder and the badger but also Jonah's height and the height and his little companion turned out to be not that strikingly disproportional (in relation to one another). Let's say, no one would think of walking hand-in-hand with a frog, even Princess Frog. Or with an elephant. For the first time during his travels, Jonah felt an interest in another being. At crossings, so the little badger wouldn't run a red light and get hit by a car. Or when a jackboot of a clumsy soldier stomped close by, Jonah shielded the little badger's bare paws with his body. He pressed himself to the body of the little animal who held the ashwood recorder. The badger walked like a little boy, hopping with delight. And naturally on his hind paws. People took Jonah and the little animal for a circus trainer with a little monkey. They passed the town's best restaurant where privileged vacationers were having a meal. Jonah felt pangs of hunger, and the little badger also asked for something, pulling Jonah by the hand and pointing with his instrument to a restaurant window.

"Yes, but first I'll sell you and then have dinner," Jonah interrupted the little animal's requests, although not very firmly.

The pet store was on Kalevi Street, in a small one-story white brick house, squeezed in between a hat store and a souvenir shop. The little pet store was favored by night cats. They found it particularly chic to leap down from the gutter of the hat store onto the roof under which guinea pigs, tortoises, and canaries were growing bored out of their minds. At this point a cat awaiting her night lover would scratch a spiteful rhythm on the roofing: "I'm free and I'm loved, and you sit there under the roof . . ." Jonah would observe these scenes when, late at night, he sometimes came into Pärnu from his forest haven. The town at night. Little heels run on granite squares. Music floats over the restaurant. Music floats in the lazy steam of the last specials of the day: shish kebabs, grilled chicken, rare steaks Suvoroff. Night tomcats leap from one roof onto another, all electric and sparkling, like night streetcars of the hometown he had left long ago . . .

Jonah knew the pet store quite well. And Aime—both manager and saleswoman—also knew Jonah.

"Tere! (The Estonian "hello"). How are you, Jonah? What did you catch this time?" Aime smiled, peeping out of her tiny half-size office where she usually sat drinking coffee with one of her girlfriends.

"Here—a baby badger. Really smart. Almost tame," Jonah answered, pushing the animal toward the counter and separating his hand from the badger's.

"Where shall I put him? He's so big." Aime seemed hesitant. But the little badger already knew where to go: straight into her tiny office.

ᏫᎶ

Jonah got so much money for the badger that he rode in a cab back to his forest, to his clearing, the place where he had spent the previous night. Almost ready to go to sleep, Jonah decided to look through his recorders, whistles, fifes, flutes, and unfinished instruments. Jonah's day had been so busy that he never had a chance to think of the most important thing. And suddenly he saw nothing but darkness in his eyes. He had left his ashwood recorder with the badger at the pet store. Sleepiness, fatigue, evening tranquility were all shaken off like dew from leaves.

Jonah was on the highway again. On the same spot where he had felt a burning desire to see Sarah, and where he saw her, all messy and barelegged, wallowing in roadside dust. Why did I let her go? Jonah thought in a moment of clarity. And then he justified himself, I had to hurry to town to sell the foundling. Some little wheels and cogs, as during the leap when music is born, began to roll in his brain and chest, ready to sprout through the tips of his fingers. They yearned to be delivered—causing chills in his scrotum and hips. On the inner surfaces of his body. Jonah even ran off to urinate behind a pine tree.

ᏫᎶ

The nighttime town, light gray in color, was making its passage to mysterious life. Smells of seaport, wine, perspiration, and cosmetics mixed and mingled in the air. Moans of the band drifted in through the open draped windows of the restaurant. Jonah walked down Kalevi Street toward the little house where animals were bought and sold. The iron clamps of the wooden shutters were locked onto iron latches. A frozen pendulum screwed up its black eyelet. Jonah's old acquaintance—one of the night tomcats—glided down onto the roof of the pet store. Jonah's first instinct was to climb to the roof and see if his ashwood recorder would call for him (through the chimney one hears the smallest noises coming from inside the house). But then he stopped. The recorder was calling him from a restaurant window. Jonah dashed there—thank goodness, he still had a whole lot of money left from the badger sale.

The hostess added an extra chair to the table where a group of sailors were having a good time. They smelled of anchovies and drank gin. The band happened to be on break; the musicians were having a bite somewhere behind the stage. The waiter's black tux reminded Jonah of the black tails he used to wear when conducting an orchestra. The restaurant menu: appetizers (caviar, herring, something else with horseradish); entrées; alcohol. You order, you pay, and you get out. Alone or with a lady, if she or you are lucky. To Jonah, the waiter resembled a conductor. Years ago, concert programs listed Jonah conducting his own music. He usually appeared at the very end of the concert; the novelty of Jonah's music shocked and electrified the audience.

The sailors threw a hundred on the waiter's tray; their boots rattled outside the windows. Jonah got his vodka carafe. The musicians returned to their seats behind the instruments. They started with a blues tune. A fat gentleman with fleshy cheeks led a half-naked high school student out to the dance floor. Actually, Jonah might have easily called her "half-dressed." A blue glittering gown covered her stomach and bits here and there. The fat gentleman and the high school girl wound up the public. Aime sat down next to Jonah. She leaned over to Jonah's brick-red neck and whispered, tickling him with her eyelashes: "A surprise is waiting for you!" The entire dining room now came into motion; after the blues the band played faster tunes: mazurka, jig, two-step, and rock 'n' roll.

"Surprise! Surprise! We want a surprise!" Aime playfully tossed her white hair; the blue torchlights of her eyes roused Jonah, stirring up his curiosity about what was coming next. He continued to empty his carafe while also pouring champagne into Aime's glass.

He kept searching around the dining room. Where was the voice of his ashwood recorder coming from?

And when the crowd dancing right in front of the band (gold saxophone, banjo, and drums) began to shout in guttural voices, "Arra! Arra! Arra!" Jonah reckoned that the surprise would turn out to be "Lezginka" or some other dance from the Caucasus. Especially when the folks at the next table were being served shish kebabs smoking like coals. But just as an iceberg only shows its very tip while concealing most of its form, the Georgian negation *arra* (no!) was only alluding to the name of the singer and triggering the enthusiasm of the crowd.

The foam of champagne mixed with the foam of Aime's hairdo. Aime jumped onto the oak restaurant table and shouted along with the crowd: "Sarah! Sarah! Sarah!"

That's what the iceberg of the singer's name both concealed and revealed.

Sarah came out to the microphone with a boy of about eight. She introduced the boy as her son whom she had lost long ago and now miraculously regained. Jonah saw his ashwood recorder in the boy's hands. Quick bilberries of the boy's eyes searched across the tables. He waved his little hand in Jonah's direction, put the recorder in his mouth, and began to play.

Translated by Maxim D. Shrayer

"Jonah and Sarah" (Iona i Sarra) was composed in Moscow, April–May 1987, one month before the author's emigration from Russia. The story is subtitled *fantella* in the original Russian; the term *fantella*—a novella with elements of fantasy— is the author's coinage. The Russian original appeared in the journal of avant-garde arts and letters *Chernovik* 7 (1992). A slightly abridged version was published in *Forverts,* the Russian-language edition of the New York *Forward* (15–21 October 1999). The present translation originally appeared in the inaugural issue of *Bee Museum* 1 (2002).

IN THE REEDS

It was a sweet little gang we had formed: Lilac, Jaws, Bow, Scalapendra, and I, Rogulya ("Cuckold," that is) or Rygulya (that is, "Belcher"), depending on the circumstances.

Every year we drag ourselves to the Reeds, where we meet up at the end of summer and stick together until the beginning of protracted autumn rains. We then disperse all over the Great Expanse until the next summer season. We don't discuss our previous whereabouts. It just isn't done among us. It might actually be unsafe. It's a rule in our midst to yield only to those reminiscences that take us back five years or more. "When the guano has mineralized," Jaws explained on one occasion. The rest of us agreed with him.

Why are we drawn to the Reeds, of all places, and why every year? Why not an alpine cave? Why not a salt mine? Or catacombs? Why not the blessedly abundant coves of the Black Sea? No, only the Reeds. The Baltic shores. Under a northern August sky. We stick around here until the tall blue globe of the sky grows dim and deflates, scratched by a stray cat of inevitability. We enjoy the metamorphosis of summer's beauty into the ugliness of the fall. And we don't suffer as much from our troubles as during the rest of the year. Premature rainfall, early mud, and the sweet longing of rotting roots of reeds make us feel content. We're not alone. It happens to others, too. All expires.

A little way off from the Reeds, sunbathers lie on yellow sand browning their bodies. They lick ice cream cones. And wallop each other with plastic balls. They wash off their sweat and sloth in the Gulf of Chukhonsk. We never join them on the beach. And we also never let anybody come near us. Scalapendra took care of that three years ago. I can still remember clearly one of the sunbathers, an obese lady with a black ponytail, squealing like a wild pig. And then the wail of the ambulance siren. Ever since that incident, a clear line of demarcation has separated the Reeds from the rest of the shore.

When we arrive in the morning—crawling, walking, or running to the Reeds from our night shelters—the sunbathers shiver and wrap themselves in their striped beach towels or bright-colored bathrobes. They don't want to be seen by us.

And only the Castle, glowing white atop the hill, makes us uneasy. We sit in the Reeds and chitchat. Frequently, we talk about legends of remote past. Sometimes we slink to the shore down a wet trail. And we never look toward the beach. The Castle hovers over the shore like a huge white cliff, ready to break off. We have a feud going on with the Castle. We detest the Castle; the sunbathers fear it. In the Castle they despise both us and the sunbathers. Though even their contempt has different shades. The Masters of the Castle see us as foul and useless. They see the sunbathers as worthless and tolerable.

Our little gang was formed between nine and twelve years ago. It's hard to find a community consisting of more dissimilar members. For instance, take Scalapendra. I knew I would start with her. But I can't help it, she's my old affection. My *femme fatale,* poisoned by love potion. And yet I'm going to step on my throat. I'll overpower myself and leave the description of Scalapendra for a better occasion. Let me start with Lilac. First, his portrait. A verbal portrait. A pitiful semblance of the truth. Lilac is always first to show up in the Reeds. He is first to reach the town of Chukhonsk. He rents the cheapest basement, which he playfully calls *bel étage*. The *bel* part comes out with particular tenderness in his pronunciation. He sings it out with his dirty lips. Three erotic letters: B-E-L. Actually, he relishes the "zh" in *étage* nearly as much. Hearing him say *bel étage*, Jaws usually spits out: "You flamboyant queen!"

I seem to have digressed a bit. Lilac is famous for the extraordinary ramifications of his veins. He seems to breathe with his skin. Like a frog. A lilac, humanoid frog. But he not only breathes with his skin. Lilac eats with his skin. His lilac capillaries absorb odors. Plenty of culinary and restroom facilities have remained in Chukhonsk since the times of . . . I think you know which times. "Money likes more money," was Jaws's favorite word of wisdom.

Prior to the formation of our society, our little gang, our brotherhood of the Reeds, Lilac (who was back then perfectly colorless) once drank a whole bottle of varnish. They revived him at intensive care. But his skin acquired a permanent coloring. During a census of the Great Expanse they didn't know how to classify him. Like a stray, Lilac joined us some five years ago, having roamed to Europe from the Far East. He used to live in the environs of Chita, making a living around pool tables in the evenings. There is a famous pool saloon in Chita. A ball would jump the cushion, and Lilac would pick it up. Chalk would crumble, he would get a fresh piece from his pocket. An empty bottle would rumble down the floor, Lilac would hide it in his bosom. People felt sorry for Lilac. He never knew his mother. Around 1937, he was found lying on a porch wrapped in rags. Why did he choose Chukhonsk? Why did he seek our company? And we—what about the rest of us? Why did we take Lilac in? Actually Lilac followed Bow. Bow came after Jaws. Jaws was trying to catch up with Scalapendra. And I saved Scalapendra from the Castle. Yes, I, Rogulya the Cuckold or Rygulya the

Belcher, depending on the circumstances. So in the end, it's no one's fault. One follows the other, men or woman alike. You may even call it fate. And promptly find a historical precedent. But it's neither fate nor precedent. Attraction. Hemotaxis. Something like a magnetic field. A purple needle pointing to the north.

But first let me tell you about Jaws. Although I really should talk about Scalapendra. She is the one of whom they say: *cherchez la femme.* She's the cause of it all. She is La. And also Scala. And La Femme, in cheerful moments. Jaws made up all these abbreviations for the woman I saved. My ex-wife. I've let go of many memories, but not this one. Swamps. Putrefaction. Take-out food counters. Public restrooms. Basements. Perspiration. I just couldn't get over her. Nor could I drive her away. The others wouldn't let me. After all, she's *La Femme.*

The biography of Jaws is very confusing. Itineraries of a traveling circus. Intricate patterns of lichens. A beehive's trajectory. These are his attributes: Iron Jaws (i.e., chews you up), Golden Jaws (i.e., a champion), Mighty Jaws (i.e., he lifts you up), Terrifying Jaws (i.e., he gnashes), Kino Jaws (i.e., he's worked in animated cartoons), and Musical Jaws (i.e., he can tap out different beats). Having performed his tricks with the circus for eleven months each year, Jaws heads for Chukhonsk and surfaces in our Reeds. He stays in Fisherman's House, and on business days he shows his tricks to groups of sunbathers. After the falling-out between La Femme and Rogulya (that is, me) over the scandal at the Castle, Jaws became even more smitten with passion for Scalapendra, but also more cautious. He kept repeating: "Better beware than get a sudden scare." As for me, I no longer care. I've cooled off toward her. I would've quit the Reeds altogether had it not been for the main secret. Which is not to say that I don't feel sorry for my weirdo friends. Including her, Scalapendra.

My passion for architecture is costing me dear. The devilish

Castle! No, not a mere block of white stone. A ship waiting at bay. Built high up over the Reeds, this ship would have to cut across to go out into the sea. That's a clever design. With extra escape options just in case. Think about it: now it stands atop the hill like a Castle, and now it leaps off across the Reeds into the Baltic Sea. Grand architecture! Mysterious design. And take a look at Scalapendra. Red-haired, even her eye lashes the color of dark gold. Like little reeds. And even her armpits are filled with gold. And all the rest. A lioness with innocently blue eyes under black eyebrows. I don't know where La Femme hides her sting. But I can testify that she is poisonous. She once stung Jaws. She also stung someone from the Castle. And she stung me. In that case I was Rogulya—"Cuckold"—that's for sure. Scalapendra has the ability to introduce different dosages: luring, terrifying, and lethal. Jaws got the luring dosage. The terrifying dosage was applied to the black-tailed woman from the beach. As for lethal . . . One hears various rumors. It's dangerous to take heed. "When the guano has mineralized," Jaws used to say.

Bow . . . You'd think we called him "Bow" because of his violin? Of course he plays the violin. A boy from a good family. The Music School of Solomon Katz. No, I beg your pardon, a different school. The one where both Busya Goldshtein and Dodya Oistrakh studied. Our Bow was educated like other wunderkinder from Deribasovskaya Street in Odessa. But he wanted an easy life for himself. He found a different application for his fiddle. He worked as a lookout during burglaries. Upon seeing danger he would change his music. A bravura piece instead of a nocturnal serenade. A dance of fire. Or something even more spirited. In reform school, Bow quickly found his way around. With older boys. How did Lilac ever spot him? Fellows like our Lilac have a flair for it. But what does Bow care? He's got ideas. While cooling off in the northern swamps he got himself ideas. He'd better play his fid-

dle. He still drags it with him to the Reeds every day. Does it for
Jaws's sake. He plays all kinds of variations for Jaws. And blades of
reeds rustle and sway in the wind. And seagulls scream. And sand-
pipers beep, keeping time. Tears stream down Lilac's venous face.
He dribbles sand on Bow's knees. And he listens. And I must sit
through this sorry drivel. Because Scalapendra fancies herself a nud-
ist. Her back is turned to the sun. And I must be there at arm's
reach. "Rogulya!" Scala calls me. And I must manage to cover her
body with a beach towel. Quickly. So that Jaws's false teeth won't
fall out of his mouth. So the music will keep on playing. And Lilac
goes on masturbating with sand. "Rogulya!" Scalapendra calls me
and I jump up—as if stung by an adder—to swathe her bodily
charms. Only her feet remain uncovered, pointing toward the sea.
Her belly button gazes at the sun. And her lips are puckered, her
tongue ever ready to sting her victim down. All this takes but a moment. Once every half hour or so, our entire gang gets aroused.
Everybody has a chance at something. I move the towel. Jaws eyes
the scene. Bow is transported with empathy. Lilac gets an erection.
And La Femme just lies on her back. Pensive, she descends into
memories. The small pyramids of her breasts. The triangle of her
armpits and pubis. Her pursed lips. I'm tired of my daily chores.
Jaws ponders life and reconstructs its events. Bow launches himself
into ratiocinations. He's got ideas. Bow discusses Martian canals
with Jaws.

"My child," Lilac gets in a word edgewise. "My dear child, there
is only one kind of canal that excites imagination." And he draws
phalluses in the sand. Phalluses are Lilac's hobby. Because of his
hobby he's been beaten up many times.

"Most entertaining, really," Jaws approves of a new variant of
canal Bow plans to dig in the Reeds.

"Plentiful fish, that's the only thing that Martians get their
nourishment from," Bow gets excited.

"Do you want to repeat here, in Chukhonsk, the Odessa of the mid–1920s?" Jaws bares his teeth.

"I hear they're talking about changes over at the Castle," Bow continues.

"Bow, you are a damn fool," I can't restrain myself any longer. "In the Castle, they want to shove off. What changes are you talking about?"

Scalapendra can't stand out scholarly debates. They infuriate her, turning her guts inside out. She also fears for me.

"To lose you, Rygulya ("Belcher," this time), is to la-la-lose everything," Jaws recapitulates, leading me out of the turf. The turf is our daily gathering point in the Reeds. "You had no business mixing whiskey with champagne. Go on. Ejaculate!"

I can understand this myself. I even understood it back when I was still a member of the Castle. Scala's cursed passion for the Architect. Who the hell was he anyhow? A mere executor of my fantellic ideas. Yes, *fantellic,* when inspiration generates mc². No atoms. No jet fuel. No solar energy. What if my wondrous talent is akin to stellar music, what then? The Masters? What about them? Oh, but it was their wish. They chose to agree with me. Did they wish to sail off? Probably. I do know for sure that neither the Masters nor the Architect possessed the gift of fantellism. Did Scalapendra have any? Look at her. There she is, lying on her back. The most solar of all women. The most ominous one. Capable of liminality.

Who is to blame? The Architect? But he's dead. Scalapendra was the prime suspect. She was detained and interrogated. In the end, we were exiled from the Castle. I was stripped of my privileges. That despite my years of service. And an immaculate reputation. She was my wife, and I vouched for her. But who actually knows what took place between her and the Architect? She's a strange girl, my La Scala. I understood one main thing: her powers were only confined to the boundaries of the Reeds. Much as I was only capable of fantellism within the boundaries of the Great Expanse. Beyond those boundaries we were just like ordinary sunbathers. And no changes from one state into another. It's as if all the fantellism gets washed off or something. Scalapendra's—outside Reeds. And mine—outside the Great Expanse. She knows it. I experienced it once in Honolulu. I gorged, I drank, I ogled. And not a stir in my head, where my third eye lies buried.

"Lovies, you're vibrating for all the wrong reasons," Lilac tries to sneak into our learned debate. "There's a rumor in my *bel étage* that the Reeds will soon be done with!"

"Rogulya!" La Femme calls me again. I'm here, ever ready to please her. Everybody gets worked up from Lilac's words. But mainly from Scalapendra's shriek. And her delicious shoulder blades on the slender stem of her backbone. Like magnolia leaves. Or blades of a small turbine in a stream. And the chiaroscuro running across her buttocks.

"This can't be. We can't live without the Reeds. Shut the fuck up, Lilac!"

"I'm only picking up the balls, dear Scala," said Lilac turned an amicably pale shade of purple.

"Oh, my God! My canals!" Bow gasped.

"Information must be reliable, otherwise it becomes misinformation," Jaws snapped his plastic teeth.

Lilac's words fell on fertile soil. At night, in my garret, La Femme snuggled up to me.

"Let's have it like we used to. All the way. Hold me tight. Don't be afraid."

No, I wasn't afraid. I knew that La's fantellism, her capacity to sting was limited to the space of the Reeds. Our garret in that old house in Chukhonsk. An overgrown apple orchard. I was holding an apple in one hand. Before La Femme's lips. With the other I was caressing her breasts. And touching them with my lips. And tasting them with my teeth.

"You my apple. Ripe juices. Me eat you. You afraid?"

"Not of you, my gadabout. Rogulya, Gulya, my Gulliver. Darling. You're my only one."

"But . . ." I wanted to ask about something else. "But what about the Reeds?"

She understood what I meant. About the other man. But she also understood the inherent truth of my question.

"You and the Reeds."

"And whom do you love more?"

She pushed her knees into my stomach and pulled me inside her.

"You the Reeds you the Reeds," she babbled while she was still able to speak, until she began to laugh and cry both together.

By morning I knew everything. Actually, to be exact, I had known of her affair with the Architect all along. One needn't be a fantellist to sense alienation or passion in a woman's eyes. I knew it for a whole year while the Castle was in the final stages of reconstruction. They were working on those parts of the design that could instantly change the Castle into a vessel, a ship capable of handling even dry terrain. The Masters were pressing to finish the construction. My fantellic talents were at a point of breaking. This was also one of the reasons why I grew indifferent toward La. And she accordingly toward me.

I'm not capable of anything during such periods, except working myself up towards a metamorphosis. Fantellism and earthly love are incompatible. But she, too, must have known that this thing with the Architect would not last very long. That it would soon pass. But the Architect had his own plans. He was taking aim. I, simple soul that I am, revealed to him the design of converting a Castle into a ship. She knew that she could not be without the Reeds. Or I without the Great Expanse. Whereas the Masters could. They had bank deposits in Switzerland. Anyway, they didn't feel at home in their own Great Expanse. As for the sunbathers, I couldn't really tell. I knew it would be over for Scala and me if the Reeds were to be destroyed. We wouldn't expire completely, but merely vegetate. Like when I was in Honolulu. Terrible memories . . .

The Architect insisted. He would hover over her knees and belly, then collapse into her.

"Find out that last bit of design from Gulliver. Then we'll get the hell out of here. All in different directions. You and I together. Rogulya to Honolulu. The Masters to Switzerland."

Thank God, I was fantellizing and didn't give in. Like glass to acid. But I was about to come out of it. And Scalapendra knew it. I was experiencing it all over, I was drawn to her again. And she struck her blow. The Architect was buried in the old town cemetery. He won posthumous laurels. A street was named in his honor. The Masters raised a howl. They were first outraged, then confused and scared. Scalapendra was expelled from the Castle. I followed her into exile . . . And now I hear about the threat that hangs over the Reeds, over our little gang. We're the last little island of dissent. Scalapendra herself is in danger. What will she do without the Reeds? I realize that our recent intimacy stemmed from this fear. So what? Love. Everything is interconnected. Every rapprochement happens for a reason. The garden at night. Apples and her breasts. And the moon. And that devilish power of fantellism in me, a power I haven't been able to realize since I followed La Femme into exile. Although I could have; I'd felt it stirring inside me. It had happened in several extreme circumstances. A little boy's legs cut off by a combine. Rain contaminated with radioactive strontium about to fall on the town. A desperate poet laureate, unable to complete a commissioned poem. In those cases I . . . I could feel it rising in me. I was fantellizing again. Saved. Saved. Saved.

Our gang was gathered at the usual spot, our turf, between a drainage ditch and a small cove, where leeches and infusoria multiply. Everyone looked grave.

"Lilac's right. The town is humming with rumors about the destruction of the Reeds," said Bow. For the first time in a succession of many summers, he didn't open his violin case.

"Little coffin with baby inside, our little orphan is sleeping," Lilac tried to cuddle up to him.

"Friends, we have been betrayed. We are in deep shit," Jaws gnashed briefly, but truthfully.

A rain cloud the color of Lilac's skin was spitting onto our turf. Scalapendra was stretched out motionless, wrapped in a piece of tarpaulin. If only she hadn't said this: "Why are you so silent, Gulliver?" If she had only remained silent. But those midnight apples, the apples we had tasted together, what were they for? The first time in many years. Nothing happens without a reason. At least in *their* opinion. But I live among them. And I'm confined to the Great Expanse.

"Where are you going, sweetums? They aren't trading Cuckolds yet," Lilac shouted behind my back. The others remained silent. Scala just lay there, motionless.

I returned to the Castle. The Masters were expecting me. Why else would a renewed pass be waiting for me? They lacked the gift of fantellism. They knew what they were doing, why and at what price. The Architect had left one little detail unfinished. Thank God! If he hadn't, that would have meant the end of the Reeds. The Castle-turned-ship would have destroyed the Reeds, moving toward the Baltic Sea. Scalapendra knew it. And she stung the Architect. But now nothing stands in my way. I had a fantellic idea. Rather than push through the reeds and smash everything on its path, the ship flies over the Reeds into the open sea. With the Masters. And me? Honolulu again? So be it. What matters is that the Reeds would be spared. They would continue to rustle and listen to Bow's violin. And Lilac sifting sand. And Jaws waiting for Le

Femme to change her position. The sunbathers won't even notice a thing. Like a young bird, the ship would leap out of the Castle. The sunbathers would be happy with an eggshell. That would maintain order. That and the legend about a fat lady with a ponytail, who had once been stung by my beloved.

Translated by Maxim D. Shrayer and Victor Terras

"In the Reeds" (V kamyshakh) was written in Moscow between 5 and 13 November 1986, as Russia stood at the threshold of political reforms that changed her destiny. Like "Jonah and Sarah" and "Dismemberers," "In the Reeds" is also subtitled *fantella* in the original. It was published in *Vremia i my* 98 (1987), three months after the author's arrival in the United States. The present translation was first published in the *Massachusetts Review* 40, no. 2 (summer 1999).

TSUKERMAN AND HIS CHILDREN

This whole story started with a long conversation in the trolley car and continued during a ride on the Moscow metro. After emerging from the underground, Tsukerman and I had a difficult time untying the knots of our entangled thoughts. He was fanatically, fervently loyal to the letter of Judaism, I—fantastically hapless in viscous conversations. Why wouldn't Tsukerman let me go, riding with me all the way to the Sokol ("Falcon") metro stop, when at home he had a wife with an advanced pregnancy and two little ones?

Our discussion had originated during a long dispute at a gathering of Jewish refuseniks, where I happened to drop a couple of lines, equally original and metaphorical, in response to Tsukerman's long deposition. The *alef* and *beit* of his talk was a certain premise, that it was senseless to engage in verbal pyrotechnics, no matter how exquisite a writer's imagery. It was pointless, he claimed, to attempt writing belles-lettres, since all the words and images *a Jew would ever need* were already prefigured in the Book. Pointless that is, because any work of literature was secondary in respect to the Book.

"Just like information stored in a computer?" I cast in a lure, testing the waters.

"Just like the truth which gives birth to multiple copies, which are nonetheless too far from—"

"—but shouldn't the Book as the original substance have a capacity to self-reproduce?" I pressed on, excited by the topic.

Here Tsukerman seized the initiative: "Yes, I'm convinced, but of the opposite, thank goodness. Not of your patchy notion," and Tsukerman flashed his monthly pass at the trolley car driver. There, in the dimly lit semicircular car of trolley No. 5, Tsukerman's philosophical meandering had begun, and it continued from the Kropotkinskaya metro station all the way to my Sokol stop. Toward the end of our ride I contemplated an act of sheer perfidy. Well, not quite perfidy, but certainly an act of bad sportsmanship. I had contemplated ascending from the subterranean hell and paradise (rumble and quietude) of the metro and hiding behind the fence of the Church of Holy Trinity, quietly waiting it out amid the graves of the departed priests and priest's wives. I had nearly committed direct apostasy so as to get away from this sticky and argumentative creature. But I couldn't. Many times, both before and after the encounter with Tsukerman, I would try to act in a way quite unimaginable for a morbidly indecisive fellow like myself. It was beyond what I was capable of.

"Okay, Tsukerman. And goodness? What about goodness? Does it also reproduce itself after one has read the Book?

"Undoubtedly. It grows out of every passage."

"And is it passed above all to the orthodox interpreters?"

"I can't believe you'd ask a thing like that? Well, what's to say? . . . You're a writer, an innovator who kills elephants not for the sake of procuring their acromegalic tusks. You need to play games, you need glamour, popularity."

"The ill-fated popularity?" I asked.

"That's right, ill-fated!" Tsukerman enhanced the rhetorical effect by pulling scornfully at his barbed-wire beard.

At this point I must offer Tsukerman's portrait. He was inharmoniously tall, like a tree which nature intends to grow big and strong but plants over the bank of a river. The tree trunk bends to the side, leaning toward the water or unable to root firmly into the ground. The curly head has already lost its vegetation and turned gnarly; the eyes are climbing up the forehead; long limbs jut out of sleeves or pants—one cannot tell. Besides, as a consequence of constantly straining his overheated mind or desiring to express himself as weightily as possible, Tsukerman would stumble in the most unexpected junctures of speech. The result sounded like a verbal puzzle, a guessing game. Tsukerman: "The function of a refusenik is to continue living in hpp . . . in hpp . . . in hpp . . ." Tsukerman silently ogles at his interlocutors as they try to complete his sentence: ". . . in hope." Tsukerman desperately waves his head, saliva bubbling at his lips, and then he finally presses out: "living in hunger and privation, but with the Book, which is the food for the Jewish spirit." Go argue with something like that! But I couldn't help it. And thank God, this time Tsukerman made an effort and pronounced the sentence clearly, reversing a seizure of his chest and jaw muscles:

"I thank you for being honest before (before yourself? before myself? before us? clearly not before the icon of Christ the Savior over the entrance to the church!) . . . before Jewry. Your popularity is so more vexing because all your fictions, shenanigans, tomfoolery, harlequinade, verbal buffoonery, hocus-pocuses, razzle-dazzle, eniki-beniki, gogol-mogols . . . all your vertiginous wordplay, are in effect rot, ashes, and vanity. Although, strange as it seems (now I'll be honest with you), my kids like it quite a bit. Especially Varvara. But you know, she . . ." Tsukerman sighed forlornly and jerked his big head in the direction of the icon of Christ the Savior, as if casting a shadow on it.

"Well, you see, finally you've said something real," I picked up the thread of conversation, glad at Tsukerman's words. "My poems, my little stories, you know they're alive with goodness and kindness. How else would I write for the kids?"

"Oh, my God, how naive you are! Your goodness, your kindness . . . they are barren. A couple of days, and it's all been forgotten. The kids will grow up and be drawn to the eternal contents of the Book. And they'll forget all about you and your little stories."

"Fine with me if they will. We all forget goodness and kindness."

What did he want with me? Why had he dragged himself all the way to the bus stop across the church square, when he had small children and a pregnant wife waiting at home? What was eating Tsukerman? Like a true stoic he struggled with himself, the way hermits in caves would fight off the devil's affronts. I thought of fitting texts to defend myself. Look, I was going to tell him, the Book honestly records that even in times immemorial things weren't as simple as you would have us believe. Far from it! Look at all those triangles of desire: Eve-Satan-Adam, or Leah-Jacob-Rachel. And how about Lot's drunk debauchery with his daughters? And Joseph whom his own brothers sold into slavery! Or King David, yes, King David, how did he gain a wife? Never mind Job the dissident. And all of this had been ground, layered over, settled, and we don't falsify or embellish these things, we don't paint with pink pastels over the pages of the Book. We don't seek goodness in the indecorous parts of the Jewish chronicle. All of this I wanted to give to Tsukerman, so he wouldn't be going around brandishing his embellished copy of the Book.

But at this point, as I was about to speak (we were waiting for bus No. 100 in a small crowd of old ladies who had just attended the vespers), a drunk beggar-invalid accosted us. No, everything I've just said about him is untrue, except "accosted us." The person who accosted was a burly vulgarian with a face steamed bright red from drinking beer laced with vodka. He would usually circulate around the Sokol metro stop: outside the food market and liquor store, near the kiosks, and most frequently in front of the church gates. Twisting his hands and legs and contorting his body, he usually succeeded in passing for a handicapped person. With his upturned hand, he would catch petty copper coins. But this time his standard act didn't come off. He was too drunk. And so he stood with the group of churchgoing old ladies and provoked them. Brazenly he spewed obscenities at the old lades who were accustomed to seeing him outside the church gates. The old ladies turned away from the beer-faced boor, but did so delicately, so as not to enrage him. Finally one of them openly expressed her annoyance:

"Making fun of old folks, the shameless devil, and just a little while ago he was begging for alms on the church steps."

But the other old ladies admonished her: "Don't speak ill of God's own person, the holy fool. So he drank too much, but that's because he's suffered. Didn't he fight the Germans for us, didn't he hurt himself defending us?"

"What makes you think he's an invalid?" the old lady continued. "All his limbs are in place, and look at his mug—it's wide like two bricks put together. And my own husband, Nikolai Ivanovich Dedyulin, never came back from the war. Yeah, and even the *pokhoronka* (death notification) I received back in '43 has turned to yellow dust," the old lady muttered, guarding herself from the fists of the drunk imposter.

Tsukerman interfered in the public argument by asking the drunk: "Comrade, please convey your philosophical concept in regard to this conflict."

Tsukerman's wondrous appearance and scholarly language stumped the drunk, rendering him speechless. A speechless beast, he became even more enraged. He dashed his huge fist at Tsukerman's face, which looked like a work of Cubo-Futurism with its asymmetrical facets and axes. But the drunk missed and instead hit a metal door hidden in the middle of an electrical pole. Something inside the door short-circuited, crackling, humming, and exploding, gushing out a cascade of yellow-green, blue-orange, and golden sparks. The electrical pole started prancing like an elephant

who had stepped onto a snake, prancing and rocking while also un-
furling like a merry-go-round. Embraced, the beggar-impostor and
Tsukerman whirled and swayed in synch with the pole, their eyes
blinking like streetlights. I caught a glimpse of the two of them sitting atop the electrical pole, their ankles and arms clinched together
. . . The old ladies—some of them dropping to the ground, others
standing in stupefaction—watched with joyous terror the unfolding
of this divine miracle. The last thing I saw from a telephone booth,
where I found refuge as I was trying both to avoid bodily injury and
to call the fire department, was a column of fire, atop of which
Tsukerman and the drunk had been catapulted into Moscow's
evening sky.

The following day newspaper reports described "the courage
of the war veteran F. F. Khrenkov, who had risked his life in order
to rescue citizen Ts-man, who ungratefully insists on emigrating to
Israel."

I would have gladly forgotten all about Tsukerman with his
phantasmagoric flight across Moscow's sky and his philosophical
impositions, had it not been for the plight of refuseniks that we
shared, the plight forcing us to go around the same narrow rink,
within the same old pavilion. I should also mention that there had
been one other event that had preceded the scandal at the bus stop
and my flight from the scene. After emerging from the underground, and before walking over to the bus stop across the church
square, Tsukerman and I had a round of debate in a shish-kebab
cafeteria. We started with table white wine. After the second bottle,
Tsukerman arranged for the waiter to serve us a 40° drink disguised
in a lemonade bottle. What was in it for Tsukerman? I really don't
know. At home, didn't he have a wife about to give birth and little
kids waiting? But I do know that after drinking three bottles, when
Tsukerman and I reached the bus stop and encountered the group
of pious old ladies, the drunk veteran-impostor, and the flaming

electrical pole, we had been rather well prepared for all sorts of phantasmagorias.

I would have tossed all this out of my head just as every day I toss various notes on scraps of paper that tend to accumulate, instead of money, in my bag, my pockets, my wallet. Believe me, I would have forgotten all about his obtrusive attempts to prove to me, a Hebrew in spirit and blood, a Jew whose mother tongue is Russian, that the Book belongs only to the chosen few. It would be fair if the Book belonged to the ones it has chosen. But no, Tsukerman would have you believe that the Book belonged to the ones who have chosen to hide behind it as though it were the Great Chinese Wall. I would have forgotten all about Tsukerman had I not been reminded of his existence. He turned out to be lucky: he was given permission to emigrate during the worst year for the refuseniks, when hardly anyone was leaving. Our refusenik community had entrusted me to help the Tsukermans with packing and suchlike arrangements. "He can't manage on his own, can he?" I was told. "His wife has just had their third child." So a group of us ended up running different errands for Tsukerman. In particular, I was put in charge of procuring plane tickets and mailing his books. At the time one needed to get a special permit at the Lenin State Library in order to take books out of the country. I was able to obtain permission to ship his engineering books to Israel. But not all of his books passed the review. I called him from a pay phone on Kalininsky Prospekt.

"Listen, Tsukerman, there's a problem with your Judaica books. I have no idea what to—"

"—my metal science books, did they pass?" Tsukerman interrupted me.

"Sure, everything except the Judaica," I repeated.

"Great! Then we're all set. Just bring them back, would you? Or, come to think of it, why don't you just keep them!"

What was left were the plane tickets. Tsukerman wouldn't even hear of economy class.

"Don't you forget, I deserve to fly to Eretz first class. I've earned it, this right, by taking risks, while others . . ."

In the end, all my tasks were completed, and I all I had left to do was to deliver the list of permitted books with the official stamp and the plane ticket into Tsukerman's hands. And then I could count the days left before Tsukerman's departure. So before breathing the air of freedom—the air of being liberated from Tsukerman's dogmatic and encroaching beliefs—I picked a day to deliver the list of books and the tickets. As for the old books on Jewish law, which the Lenin State Library refused to allow Tsukerman to take to Israel, I gave them to Monya Kalman, a fervent advocate of rooting Jewish culture in Russian statehood. Kalman was a nice old man, but his ideas were just as nonsensical as Tsukerman's, in my view.

Tsukerman lived in the Sviblovo district of Moscow, in a pink-and-white structure. His apartment building stood in a row of monstrous creations of Soviet architecture of the epoch of stagnation. These pink-and-white structures stood guard over the high bank of the Yauza River, awaiting the arrival of the long-promised epoch of "developed socialism" that would sweep them away. It would sweep them away, and then Moscow's new ethnic population would move into their new dwellings, built in place of the pink-and-white structures and washed in blood and darkness. Some of the former residents of the neighborhood would emigrate and be dispersed throughout the world, just like Tsukerman, who was now leaving for Israel.

"How about a glass of tea?" Tsukerman asked me, fingering the tickets for the umpteenth time while rolling the thick wheels of this spectacles down the list of books I brought over. "You might have been pushier with them, but I'm nonetheless grateful for all your troubles," he concluded gravely.

"Some tea would be nice," I reminded him of his offer after a minute or two of barren silence.

"Varvara, Varya," Tsukerman called out.

The door to one of the bedrooms opened ("The nursery," Tsukerman explained), and a girl of about nine or ten slowly waded into the living room, her tummy stuck out so as to balance the weight of her heavy newborn brother she was carrying.

"What do you need, papa?" she asked raising her round face at Tsukerman.

"Some tea . . . Well, I guess I can do it myself, since you're with the children," Tsukerman replied in a passive-aggressive way.

I noticed that Tsukerman was agitated but also strangely disinclined to engage in philosophical arguments. In addition to her baby brother, Varya was also taking care of a three-year-old boy, who had attached himself to the hem of her dress and was playing choo-choo train. Puffing and honking, he imitated the steam and the rattling noises of the wheels: "Huff-huff-huff . . . Choo-choo-choo . . . Clank-clank-clank . . ."

"This is Barukh," Tsukerman said to me. "Barukh, come say hello to Mr. Writer," Tsukerman called his son who was busy playing choo-choo train. The boy came up to the table and stood there, waiting.

"Boris-Barukh, do you remember the poem about the choo-choo train?" I asked, trying to make contact with Tsukerman's boy. (*Boris* is the common Russian equivalent of the name "Barukh").

"Come on, Barukh, answer Mr. Writer. He's written all sorts of things for children," Tsukerman demanded. "Didn't you read it with your sister Varya?"

"Little puffing choo-choo train," Barukh-Boris squeezed out and stopped.

"Go on!" Tsukerman yelped.

"Little huffing choo-choo train, where're you taking me again? Past the church's onion dome, from my sister, from my home . . ." Varya recited in her brother's stead and burst into tears. The baby in his sister's arms woke up, disturbed by the quakings of her tummy that had replaced her gentle rocking. The baby woke up and started tossing and squealing. Then Barukh-Boris-the-choo-choo-train started honking, and a fountain of tears squirted from his dark-gray sorrowful eyes.

"Take away Barukh! Put Samuil to sleep! Take away put to sleep leave us alone. Now!" Losing control, Tsukerman tumbled into his chair and started gulping his tea and dipping a vanilla biscuit into his glass while shaking the crumbs off his barbed-wire beard with a rumpled old handkerchief.

"And where's your wife?" I asked Tsukerman.

"Oh, don't even go there! Well, actually, an *engineer of human souls* like yourself . . . You understand. My elder child, the girl, you know I've adopted her. De facto, that is."

I said nothing in response. What was I to say? I'd seen all sorts of somersaults of destiny.

"I don't need to tell you what it's like raising children in my position as a refusenik. I mean, in *our* position. My meager earnings. And my wife couldn't work at all! But we're in love, in love! To make the long story short, Varya's father used to support her financially. But now we're stuck. Hit the wall. He's got the right of veto, like a member of the Roman senate."

"So what have you decided?" I asked.

"To cross the Red Sea, right now, before the servants of the pharaoh have turned my children into slaves."

"All of your children?"

"Why must you put it this way!? No one's asking you."

"I apologize, Tsukerman, it's your private business. I shouldn't have said anything in the first place."

"You think it's easy? I'm going crazy here. You know Varvara is

like a daughter to me. But what can I do with this *barbarian,* her father?" Mouthing the word *barbarian* (*varvar* in Russian), he stressed
the bond connecting Varvara and her non-Jewish father. "How can
I fight this man? My wife is now at his place, begging him, not for
the first time, to allow . . ."

Tsukerman pulled his head into his shoulders and stared into
the wall, rocking in his chair and whining a mournful melody. The
place on the wall where his glance had frozen was a photograph of
Tsukerman's wife posing with the newborn Samuil, and on both
sides of her chair—Varya and Boris-Barukh.

"You're a writer, so tell me, what should I do if her barbarian
father doesn't give Varya permission to leave?"

ᵒᵐᵐᵒ

I would have been better off taking leave of this sad story without knowing the ending. I shouldn't have returned the calls of those
fellow refuseniks who asked me to help Tsukerman and his family.
No, better yet, would that I hadn't met Tsukerman. That's right, I
wish . . . I wish I hadn't! How many times can I keep saying this and
then repeating the same mistakes?

The morning of Tsukerman's flight I found myself in Moscow's
Sheremetyevo Airport. Twilight behind the huge windows. Twilight and the roars of landing and takeoff. A group of us seeing
Tsukerman off went up some stairs, then down some black rubbery
ribs. Then we all waited for the arrival of Tsukerman and his family.
Then boarding was announced for the flight to Vienna. Standing
next to me was a middle-aged lady, also a refusenik, who was seeing
the Tsukermans off. The lady nervously twisted a plastic bag with
some things she had prepared for Tsukerman's kids—sweets, toy
trinkets; I didn't really catch a good glance. Lost in my thoughts, I
didn't even get a chance to say a proper good-bye to Tsukerman,
and then it was too late, Tsukerman had already stepped out of the

crowd. Gesticulating vigorously, he was presenting his papers to the customs officials. On the other side of the turnstile stood Tsukerman's wife, hardly recognizable in a thick black shawl concealing her head. Baby Samuil slept in the arms of Tsukerman's wife. In one hand she clutched the handle of a green suitcase on wheels, and to the other Boris-Barukh had attached himself, playing choo-choo train.

Translated by Maxim D. Shrayer

Written in Providence, Rhode Island, in the spring of 1989, "Tsukerman and His Children" (Tsukerman i ego deti) was published in Russian in *Evreiskii mir* (Jewish World) 42 (24 January 1997). Its publication caused a polemic about varieties of Jewish assimilation and self-hatred in the pages of Jewish-Russian press in the United States and Israel. The present translation was commissioned for this collection.

DISMEMBERERS

It remained for me to place her beautiful body into the black leather case littered with early bird-cherry blossoms, and to wipe off a few unwanted tears with the sleeve of my shirt. I had decided to give my Olympia away. My thirty years of affection. My passion. The sole witness of my flights and falls. She to whom I entrusted my innermost thoughts, compressed into a line of poetry or extended into a short story. I used to take her with me wherever I went: deep into the Belorussian countryside, to Lithuania, to a cabana on the shores of the Black Sea, to Leningrad, to Siberia, to Tbilisi . . . I can't even recall all the places! And no matter how hard my writer friends begged me to let them have her, to sell her, to exchange her for another one, younger, fancier, more submissive, I never yielded to their requests.

And here I am leaving her with somebody, as I leave Russia forever.

I had waited for this hour for almost nine years. I had been preparing myself for this leave-taking. But now . . . It turned out that taking leave of her was neither simple nor safe. Not simple for me. Nor safe for my friends. "But about this later . . ." as the poet Khlebnikov said in real life or the novelist Dostoevsky through his characters.

And so I placed her into her black leather case. A wooden case bound in black leather. To be on the safe side, I girded the case with a black leather belt with an old-fashioned buckle. I think I got this time-wrinkled belt from my grandfather, a talented businessman. A Merchant of the First Guild before the Revolution, a private entrepreneur during the years of the New Economic Policy. When my grandfather gave it to me, this strip of Moroccan leather with an ancient blackened silver clasp was all that was left of his property, the rest confiscated.

We plunged into the back seat of a cab. She nestled up to me. I sensed the warmth and delicacy of her body through the layers of wood and leather that separated us. My decrepit jeans did not count as a layer owing to the superconductivity of any kind of pants separating two bodies. The driver was looking askance at his rearview mirror: why is this jerk stroking a leather case and wiping off his tears?

My friends lived in a tower. A high-rise tower of white stone. Top floor. Matvey grew orchids. Rozalinda bred canaries. They were amazing people, those friends of mine. It goes without saying that growing orchids and breeding canaries in our northern latitudes is an act of sainthood. Like cultivating a friendship with me, let it be said. A few days earlier they had called me. Just in case, they used a public phone. They called to tell me they would drop in for half an hour. This is when they offered to give her shelter in their tower. Amid orchids and canaries. I gratefully accepted their offer. There was no other choice. Taking her through customs would have been suicidal. The officers inspecting her would have recognized after a quick glance that all my infectious stories and poems had passed through her delicate fingers. They would have arrested her immediately, and detained me for "further questioning."

I left my beloved with Matvey and Rozalinda.

When my plane landed in Honolulu, I received an aerogram from my good friend, the novelist Gerd Safirov, with an account of everything that had happened during the past two weeks, since I had left Moscow. Oh yes, between leaving Moscow and arriving in Honolulu, I had treated myself to Viennese pastries, feasted on spaghetti with *frutti del mare,* had chased wild Maltese goats, as well as attempted to find a statistical differential between the Pillars of Hercules and what had remained of Lot's disobedient wife.

Gerd Safirov wrote that my beloved had not wished to hide in Matvey and Rozalinda's storage closet. She shed her case, like a lobster discarding his armor, and hobbled into the kitchen. At the time, Matvey was grafting a cutting from a lascivious New Zealand orchid onto the stem of a virgin orchid from New Orleans. She came in hobbling like a rattleturtle on her short rubber legs. A rattleturtle? It seems there are rattlesnakes, not turtles. My beloved was rattling with all her keys and levers and also ringing her little bells, like a streetcar. Matvey was dumbfounded with amazement and terror. So much so that he ended up grafting the cutting to an ironing board instead. Rozalinda dropped the egg of a pink canary that had been meant to be hatched by an orange canary (an experiment!).

"Hold it! Where are you going?" yelled Matvey, seeing that my typewriter was headed for the door.

"She must be pining for him," Rozalinda concluded. A telltale tear fell on the broken pink eggshell.

"Maybe the two of you will go pine together?" Matvey suddenly became jealous of me.

"Dummy, nobody comes back from Honolulu."

"Oh yes! I forgot! He's supposed to send me seeds of Honolulu orchids."

"And me . . ." Rozalinda stopped herself short.

My beloved had bumped her forehead against the exit door and was impatiently rattling her carriage. Her bells were ringing up a trill. Her keys were shooting like *mafiosi* caught in a drug raid.

"Would you believe it! She's crazy, rabid," Matvey commented.

"Of course she's crazy," Rozalinda agreed. "Like master, like typewriter. How good a writer is he anyhow?"

"That's why they never printed his stuff here," said Matvey, throwing more chestnuts into the fire.

"He's off to Honolulu, and we have to deal with his treasure," Rozalinda rejoined him.

"The apple doesn't fall far from the tree!" Matvey chimed in.

"Crazy geese, crazy cracklings!" Rozalinda repeated her late father's favorite saying.

"Like rabbi, like shul!"

"As the needle goes, so does the thread!"

"The wise man likes it clear, the fool likes it stupid!"

"A fool seeks a fool's company!"

"One stupid cow led all others to Macao!"

"You're a fool!"

"I hear it from a dumb ass!"

ᏮᎲᏋ

My typewriter knocked open the door and reached the lobby when Matvey and Rozalinda got up from the kitchen floor, rather rumpled and tired out by their fight, followed by as steamy a reconciliation.

"Let's go, Rollie!" Matvey proposed lazily. "Rollie" was his tender diminutive of Rozalinda.

"You go, Mafik, I'm not dressed." Rozalinda playfully pushed her husband to the door.

Matvey caught up with her near the elevator, when she was just about to jump in after a neighbor's dachshund. The neighbor, Vassily Fomich, who happened to be there on the occasion of the national holiday, Meliorator Day, asked Matvey: "Neighbor, let me pet your jewcupine." Vassily Fomich came up with "jewcupine" because of the typewriter's keys, sticking out like porcupine's quills. And because like myself, my friends Matvey and Rozalinda were of Jewish stock.

My beloved was tied up again and locked in the storage closet.

Yet they didn't want to offend me, since I too had been locked up by the authorities and kept in detention. What if all of a sudden I found out that they kept her in a closet and decided not to send them plant seeds and canary eggs from Honolulu? My friends began to refer to the closet as "guest room."

"How's our Olympia doing in the guest room?"

"Seems she's calmed down."

"She's got quite a temper."

"Exactly like him."

"You seem to be sad about something!"

"No smoke without a forest fire!"

"Would I have somebody to pine after?"

"You just gave yourself away!"

"I couldn't care less!"

"Watch it, woman!"

"Why don't you just shut up!"

ᏬᎳᏇ

When they woke up, Olympia was tearing the last sheet of wallpaper from the bedroom wall, rolling the paper through her black tongue-carriage, and finishing the typing of a humoresque from the life of a Jewish dissident-refusenik, the designer Arkady Blyachman. In her story, Blyachman was almost drowned in cement mix by his coworkers. Arkady had been demoted to this menial job because he wouldn't cooperate with the authorities. The drunken proletarians made several attempts on his life, unable to drown their inferiority complex in vodka and projecting it on Arkady. Olympia was about to finish her narrative, wondering if she might type something else on the bedroom's satin curtains. She wasn't sure how to cut them.

"Into the forest!" Matvey roared like a madman. He woke up first.

"Florist, oh my florist!" Rozalinda jumped up in bed, dreaming of an Übermensch florist in love with her.

"Calm down, it's her again," said Matvey, pointing at the domestic printing press at work.

"I am calm," moaned Rozalinda, nearly fainting.

"Again a story with a subversive topic, just like what her owner used to write before going to Honolulu."

"We'll burn the wallpaper and bury Olympia," Rozalinda said, recovering her senses.

"That's what I said: into the forest!" Matvey put on his overalls.

"Call a cab," Rozalinda suggested.

"Idiot, they'll follow us," Matvey objected.

"A fool may get the right idea in spite of herself," Rozalinda quoted a Russian classic.

They dragged their feet to the train station. Matvey carried my beloved Olympia, encased and tied with a belt. Rozalinda carried a shovel. They got off at Snegiri ["Bullfinch"] Junction, and headed for an old rowanberry tree whose savory berries they harvested for preserves every fall. Under the rowanberry tree stood a bearded character with a pocketknife. He was either dismembering somebody or cutting himself a whistle. They returned to the station and traveled as far as Istra. Then, by bus, they went to New Jerusalem monastery. They secretly dug a grave at the monastery graveyard and buried Olympia. A different bearded character, not the one with the pocketknife who was either dismembering or cutting something, but a monk, accosted them at the Istra station.

"You can't bury someone without a cross and a prayer. Besides, you haven't paid for the plot, and you aren't Russian Orthodox."

They exhumed Olympia, paid the monastery a fine, and brought her back home. Exhausted, they kept repeating one verb, "dismember, dismember, dismember," a sublimated product of meeting the bearded character with a pocketknife, and of Rozalinda's Freudian nightmares.

At night, Matvey made a round hole in the hood of an abandoned vehicle—the cheap metal yielded to a can opener. He removed the battery and carried it to his tower. The sulfuric acid from the stolen battery devoured the typewriter's delicate fingers, broken off by my dear friends Matvey and Rozalinda. Levers, wheels, rolls, bell, and pedal were dumped into garbage bins all over the neighborhood.

"Try to catch the wind!" Matvey uttered, enjoying a quiet dawn for the first time in days.

"The end crowns the good work," purred Rozalinda.

"And your pinkie has news for you," Matvey playfully hinted to an egg just laid by the canary.

"You haven't grafted a cutting in a long time, Mattie," Rozalinda seconded him.

"Nobody returns from Honolulu," Matvey said, embracing his wife.

"She won't bother us anymore," Rozalinda smiled.

Translated by Maxim D. Shrayer and Victor Terras

The author wrote "Dismemberers" (Raschleniteli) in his Moscow apartment between 21 and 30 May 1987, while a CBS crew, headed by Dan Rather, filmed a segment of an hour-long special about the USSR. The special, *The Soviet Union: Seven Days in May,* was aired in the United States in the summer of 1987 and featured the actual prototype of Olympia, the typewriter in the story. Shrayer-Petrov, his wife Emilia, and his son Maxim emigrated from Russia on 7 June 1987. Subtitled *fantella* in the original, "Dismemberers" was subsequently reworked twice, in 1989 and 1993, and a revised version appeared in *Vestnik* (25 August 1992). The present translation originally appeared in *Southwest Review* 85:1 (2000).

DAVID AND GOLIATH

But why don't you judge for yourself . . .

David was told to stand to the right of the turnstile. The right side was designed to allow passage or block the way—that is, together with its other side, the left. Both sides looked like hands with rounded plastic stumps. David was waiting for Mama, clinging to her black shiny bag. Actually, he held it by the handles. The bag was his and Mama's only property. Their horse and cart at the same time. Mama had been led away by customs officials for a private examination—after all of Aunt Masha's and Uncle Volodya's abundant kisses. Finally, after being prodded by a host of mustachioed, bearded, and spectacled faces, he and Mama passed through the first turnstile. Their documents were checked, and some things were shaken from the bag: Mama's cosmetics, oranges, and something else, probably a little bologna sandwich.

"Taking such a little one away to the Zionists," a customs officer grumbled under his breath. He was dressed in a gray military uniform with little stars attached to his shoulder straps. Mama silently looked at David, as if reminding him: "Don't answer them." At home, when they were about to leave for the airport to fly from Moscow to Vienna, Mama had warned David, "Just be patient, no matter what. Just try. Their job is to search people. They trust no one. Particularly not you and me, David. So please be patient. Freedom is almost here."

David knew what patience was. He and his Mama had been waiting for eight years. Waiting and suffering. Actually, Mama had been suffering for eight years. David, for five. Because until the age of three he didn't know what it was to suffer, to wait, to believe in miracles.

At first the three of them had lived together—Daddy, Mama, and David. He didn't remember that, of course. But Mama told him about it. The three of them had lived together until David turned one. A year—it's a lot and a little. Little for David. But for Daddy? Then Daddy was sentenced. He had been inciting refuseniks to participate in demonstrations along with dissidents. Later he started to write leaflets. And copy them on some machine. Mama called it "xerox." Like zero. Something cold. Blood-stirring. White with black wrinkles. It looked like dirty snow. Daddy got seven years of prison, and five of exile. David remembered these numbers, because they Mama repeated them many times to different people: to their friends—refuseniks all—as well as guests from America, Canada, England, and France. The visitors came, bringing them little things. Chewing gum and candy bars for David. And each time, before the visitors offered their presents, Mama would tell them Daddy's story, in detail: about his political activities, his arrests (in the beginning, only for a day at a time), how he got caught with leaflets printed on xerox. But Mama never, ever came close to what was most important. *That* she only spoke about with Aunt Masha and Uncle Volodya—about how Daddy had been caught. There were whispered words: "finked," "stooge," "KGB men," and other such things. All the complexity of what had gone on with Daddy was revealed only to Aunt Masha and Uncle Volodya, because they weren't visitors but Mama's own people.

Later, when David turned six, a letter from Daddy came from the prison hospital. He wrote that he had broken a hip and that Mama would be allowed to visit him. Leaving David at Aunt Masha's and Uncle Volodya's, she flew to Siberia. David thought that Mama would return soon, but she didn't. He waited and waited. He even began to feel some anger toward his Daddy: why wouldn't he let Mama come back home? "Be patient, David, Mama hasn't forgotten about you. There's been some kind of complication. Mama is needed there." Uncle Volodya took David for rides around Moscow and they even went to the circus and the zoo.

Mama returned in the spring, when they had learned almost all the alphabet in David's kindergarten class—up to the letter "T." It was preparation for elementary school. "T" especially tormented David. Before falling asleep on the eve of Mama's homecoming, he had turned over in his mind all the words starting with "T." The way their teacher required, everything memorized. David lay on the sofa in Aunt Masha and Uncle Volodya's living room. Listening to the whooshing cars that flattened the snow on Gorky Street, he remembered the words: "trumpet," "tires," "ties," "train," "Toby." Daddy was a trumpeter; they drove him away to prison in a car with big beastly tires; there are many, many ties a train must cover to take David to Daddy. And he wanted badly to cry when Toby—who lived with Aunt Masha and Uncle Volodya—licked his nose: "Better sleep. Tomorrow is a new day."

The next day Mama came home. David found out about it in the evening. Why hadn't Mama picked him up from the kindergarten the minute she got back? Was she afraid that David wouldn't recognize her? Mama was wearing a black dress with a flounce that trailed like a tail. Again words starting with "T." Mama had darkened and withered. Of course David recognized Mama, but there was a lot in her he didn't recognize. Before leaving for the prison hospital, Mama had never wasted a minute. She was always busy with something: cooking, sewing, typing, discussing Daddy's problems with friends. Now she would sit quietly in a chair by the window that overlooked Gorky Street in Aunt Masha's and Uncle Volodya's apartment. She sat, looking through pictures of Daddy.

ᏇᎿᏋ

They were lodged in Frau Eva's hotel. Not far from Vienna, in the small town of Gablitz. Mama and David's little room was located right under the roof—in the attic. David lay, his eyes closed tight, trying to remember all the incredible events of the day: Shereme-tyevo Airport in Moscow, the custom officers, and a border guard who had stared at David for quite a while before he let him go. "Now we are free, sweetheart," Mama said, and she started to cry. "And Daddy . . ." She stopped, but David knew that Daddy had been left behind for good, in Siberia. In the prison cemetery. Try-ing not to fall asleep amid such sad thoughts, David listened closely to the noise of the highway, running right below their attic room. The noise was light, merry, mischievous—like the noise of a skating rink or a waterfall.

In the morning they went down to the dining room, where Frau Eva treated new emigrants to a "continental breakfast." The words:"continental breakfast, continental breakfast" could be heard at many tables. And this "continental breakfast" sounded particu-larly amusing when discussed by elderly folks who hailed from the south of Russia or from Ukraine and spoke funny Russian. "Frau Eva," "continental breakfast," and another one—"collect call." Especially "collect." This word was constantly in the air. After rolls and coffee with milk and jam, David became very excited, and the new words amused him too. Frau Eva, continental breakfast, and collect. Mama told the people sharing the table with them all the details of their escape, about Daddy, about customs officers. Now she didn't have to worry about anything. There were friends all around—all former refuseniks, like David and herself. A loud bunch of them was sitting at the next table. It was clear that they had been here for a while already, so relaxed did they feel in Frau Eva's hotel. They talked in a peculiar way, which was at first totally puz-

zling to David, because so many of their Russian words were pronounced incorrectly. And it became even more fun when he began
to understand the words. He started playing a game with himself:
deciphering some of the words they said.

A huge, greasy, bristly-faced fellow seemed to David the most
remarkable of all. He had long since finished his coffee and rolls
with jam and was now starting in on a smoked pork leg. He gnawed
around this pork leg, repeating greasy words, "Piggy-wiggy, juicy
piggy-wiggy, I'm gonna swallow you, that's right, swallow, swallow,
swallow . . ." Then he forgot about "piggy-wiggy" and only repeated "swallow." It was as if he were gnawing not a pork leg but a
tiny swallow, while dipping an onion into salt. The funniest thing
was that his wife—a sleepy, swollen-faced plump woman, with tousled, colorless hair—was tenderly stroking the fellow's back, repeating, "Gosha, Gosha, eat Gosha, eat dear heart." David was so taken
by the scene that he stared quite impolitely at the man and his wife.

"Hey, wanna finish it?" the fellow with the pork leg addressed
him.

"Thank you, I'm not hungry," David answered courteously. He
turned away.

The fellow, however, wanted to have some more fun. He got
up, wiped his greasy hands against his faded sweat pants and plopped
down next to David.

"What's your name, buddy?" the fellow breathed an onion
belch at David.

"David."

"And I'm Gosha. What's up?"

All sorts of things always came to David's mind. And now, as
soon as the guy called himself Gosha (a diminutive of Igor), David
gave him the nickname "Goliath." Certainly he didn't say it out
loud. But he thought about it—that's how big and wild the guy was.
Aunt Masha would have called Goliath "wild and overgrown." He

was still staring at David, trying to fish some idea out of his shaggy head—fogged by all the pork fat he had consumed—and connect it somehow with the newcomers. Not finding anything suitable, he became enraged with himself; he breathed heavily, burping louder and louder. Then Frau Eva, who didn't let anyone touch the phone without her permission, shouted, "Novikoff—Telephone—Boston!" Mama had kept her maiden name.

"Hear that, Roza, this new one is Novikoff, a Russian name," Goliath barked. Then he roared with laughter, sure that his joke had hit home.

"No kidding, I got it right off," Roza replied. "All these *goyim* come here on our Jewish money."

"Shame on you!" interrupted an old lady with neat white curls, on her way to Chicago, where she had a son. Mama had helped the lady with her suitcases at the airport. "There is a child here!" the old lady said right into Roza's sleepy face.

"Hey you, vermin. Shut up! This is the Free World. We talk like we wanna talk," Goliath yelled at the old lady.

Taking David's hand, she led him from the dining room.

David said nothing about it to Mama. And he forgot about Goliath and his Roza as soon as Mama told him about her telephone call to Sasha Fuchs, a friend of Daddy's. Sasha Fuchs had agreed to be their sponsor; he would send out the necessary papers soon. "Sponsor" was another new word, like "Frau Eva," "continental breakfast," and "collect." David managed to keep Goliath out of his mind for almost the entire day, because everything was so tasty and exciting. At the nearest supermarket, *Markt-Billa*, Mama and David bought all kinds of fantastic goodies. They went up an asphalt road—passing pretty houses—straight into the forest. Sitting on a very wide stump, they ate one thing after another: chocolate custard, bananas, peaches, and ham with tasty, porous bread. And drank real Coca-Cola. Or maybe the order was different: ham, bread and tomatoes, then sweets with fruit.

"It's no accident that Daddy used to call me 'squanderer,' " Mama said.

"Have you spent all our dollars?" David became frightened.

"Oh no, honey, only a few," Mama smiled.

They were in the very famous Vienna Woods, Wienerwald. Large, long-nosed birds sang for all they were worth. "Song-thrushes," Mama explained. When they were passing a glade near a creek, Mama found ramsons. She also found mint on the roadside. They picked some ramsons and mint. Mama knew a lot about forests. Before they became refuseniks, she had been a graduate student at the Timiryazev Academy of Agriculture. Song-thrushes. Goliath. Something rolled in David's memory. He was remembering. Of course, it had nothing to do with thrushes. Yes, yes. He remembered: back in their Moscow yard, adjacent to the Timiryazev Park, some boys claimed to have shot down crows with slingshots. "I'm the best, I can kill a crow with one shot," Mishka Kutov was the biggest braggart of all. David shivered, so much did Mishka Kutov resemble Goliath. Tousled. With greasy lips, always noshing on a cookie. Ever ready for a fight. Now Goliath wouldn't leave him alone. Not even in Wienerwald.

◦◦◦

They returned to the hotel in the evening, but didn't stop in the dining room. They ate some cookies and drank milk in their attic room. Wonderful cookies, shaped like dumbbells and dipped in chocolate. David fell asleep right away. He heard neither the pulsating highway, nor the night birds, nor the creaking of the door as it opened and shut. He awoke in complete darkness. Wanted to pee. He always wanted to pee when he drank milk before bed. At home it was easy. The bathroom was to the right of his room. But here? It would be a pity to have to wake Mama up. She was sleeping so silently in her bed. Tired out. It was good that she hadn't heard Goliath's terrible jokes. David tried to fall asleep again, tossing in bed and fighting off the urge. At last, unable to hold it any longer, he fully awoke and called, "Mama, Mommy! I have to pee." His hand groped about to find the nightstand between their beds. He stepped on the floor. "Mama, wake up, please." He examined Mama's bed with his hands and, scared, pressed them to his tummy, which only intensified his urge. Mama wasn't in the room, but the thought that something had happened to her was blunted by his tormenting fear of doing something shameful right here, in his room in the hotel. It hadn't happened to him in such a long time. David pushed open the door and made his way to the corridor. He remembered the bathroom being somewhere at the end of the corridor and moved on, like a blind man, his fingertips sliding along the wall. He found a door. He remembered: this one led to the stairway. Half-opening, the door sang in a high-pitched voice. He passed the door and someone's room, when a raucous laugh and then Mama's tender giggle bounded up from the stairway. Mama's giggle, somewhere out of the stairway's jaws. He even imagined Mama—slender, her straw-colored hair cut short. Scared, she was staring out of the jaws lined with step-teeth. Then suddenly— laughter. It meant that someone else, a second person, whose laughter sucked in Mama's giggle, had made her feign excitement. David was ready to believe that it was the sharp-teethed stairs themselves that both laughed and tortured. He shoveled ahead until he found the bathroom, and then relieved himself.

What he had to do now was to get Mama out of trouble. He went back to the stairway and quietly descended two or three steps. There was no more of Mama's giggle or the rude laughter. "You are such a dreamer, David," he was about to repeat Mama's favorite saying, when he heard the same deadly and obnoxious voice, but now it wasn't laughing—it was trying to persuade.

"We only live once, you know. Shouldn't we skim off some of the cream? Come on." Goliath's voice, David was sure: the voice of ugly Goliath. And Mama's—not protesting, not struggling to free itself from the stairway-basement voice, but softly dissuading, "Oh no, Gosha. You've got family. Roza and the kids." David couldn't stand it. But he didn't know what to do. Mama wasn't in any danger. He found himself in the most absurd situation: he had eavesdropped on a private conversation. He ought to return to his room immediately. He went back upstairs, thinking that he had acted according to the rules common in their family, but feeling at the same time, with all his guts, in his tummy and tiptoes, that he was betraying someone.

The next day Mama wrote letters to Moscow. David read. The old lady with white curls—Mme. Yakobson—gave him a book of Bible stories for children. Soon he ran across the story of David and Goliath. But of course! It was not by chance that something had stirred in him, halting him. It may have been Grandpa Boris—Daddy's father—from whom he had heard it before. The legend about the little shepherd David, who slew the cruel giant Goliath with a slingshot. Or perhaps not with a slingshot. In the story the weapon's name was different. But it was all the same. David clearly visualized the little shepherd putting a stone into the leather thong of his slingshot, stretching the rubber bands and then . . . Goliath falls down, stricken dead! Falls down on the land he yearned to enslave.

Earlier that morning David had noticed an old rubber bicycle tube; Frau Eva's grandson, Günter, had thrown it away. In the hazel grove—it was on the other side of the highway, near a glade—David chose a branch with two firm shoots sticking out. He broke it off and went back home. Instead of a leather patch, he used a piece of tarpaulin he had also found behind the hotel, in a trash heap.

"What are you doing there, David?" Mama asked, not lifting her head from her letter.

"Nothing. Just playing war. Could you give me some thread, please?"

ᏼᎦᎦᏜᎩ

The next day, after the continental breakfast, David and Mama went to sunbathe. In Gablitz everybody sunbathed at the town pool. For a fee. They lay on chaises, licking fruit popsicles, and from time to time dove into the water. It was cold and sky-blue—blue from the paint that covered the pool's walls and the blue tiles on its bottom. At first Mama tried to draw David's attention away from the topless young ladies who stood and walked by the pool. Finally she gave up, laughing, "That's the fashion here, honey."

"The rules are different here, right, Mommy?" David asked.

Mama didn't answer. She sent him to get another popsicle, "Buy a different flavor!"

As David was walking back (he was away for five or six minutes, because the Austrian boys and girls continually ran to buy popsicles and chose their flavors slowly) he bumped into Goliath, who was hurrying to the exit. "Why did he come?" David thought. But soon he forgot about Goliath—he was watching a girl in thin panties do a somersault as she dove into the water.

David and Mama had hot dogs for lunch. Mama boiled them quickly. She tried not to be long in the kitchen that was ruled by Roza, Goliath's wife, and was crowded with Jewish women. The compassionate old lady—the one going to her son's in Chicago—was among them.

"Thanks, hot dogs will do fine for us," Mama explained to the old lady, who was trying to convince her of the necessity of "giving the child high-calorie food." They ate hot dogs with tomatoes and drank Fanta. David took some up to their room—he liked to sip it through a straw. He sat on his bed, reading. The new legend was about King Solomon, son of King David, the shepherd-turned-king. The one who built the Great Temple. Mama went to the post office to mail letters to Russia. Everybody said "Russia," "from

Russia," "to Russia," although most of the emigrants came from Ukraine.

David read the part of the story in which the Queen of Sheba uses all her charms to get Solomon to marry her. And though she did become his wife for a short time, King Solomon managed to make fun of her: he made her walk on a mirror so that everyone could see her hairy legs. This part of the story seemed very unclear to David. Why marry if all you want to do is laugh at hairy legs?! He stopped reading and went for a walk—the reading gave him a headache.

A girl in white shorts smiled as she bicycled toward David. "Hello!" he shouted, waving a hand after the girl. A song-thrush climbed on the finial of a little brown house and trilled an intricate tune. Large yellow daisies grew and grasshoppers chirped on both sides of the road going up the hill into Wienerwald. David rushed after one of the grasshoppers and almost caught him, but the chirping vanished at the edge of a potato field. David wandered up the looping road as it slowly crawled into the mountains. A few days before, he had walked this way with Mama. Blue, white, and mother-of-pearl cars had slid somewhere below him, suddenly reappearing on the highway as if from nowhere. He walked past a mysterious abandoned house with white angels adorning the window frames. A pond breathed its chillness. A windmill's webbed wings rustled. Then he passed a ditch, heady with mint growing nearby. The glade with ramsons. The slingshot jangled in David's pocket. The pebbles knocked against each other. David remembered that last time the road had led them to a meadow, dark-green with thick grass. Here was the meadow again, there the scarlet poppies, like little blood-spots. Blood? He hadn't shot at anybody. It was so peaceful: birds, very tall hornbeams, elms, and poppies.

In a distant corner of the meadow—closer to the bushes—David saw a bear's head: brown, tousled, rocking and swaying. He felt cold and then something clenched at his groin. The slingshot was in the right pocket of his pants. David backed up silently and, on tiptoes, skirted the meadow. He couldn't see the bear's muzzle through the thick grass, but the back! The lower part of the bear's back was hairless, like a pig's. And this lower part lived its own life: it breathed, swung, moved up and down, as if trampling someone into the grass. David squatted and came closer to the strange animal, loading the slingshot with a pebble. A chink opened in the grass, and horrified, he saw that the animal's head belonged to Goliath. Underneath this head Mama's head coiled, as she moaned and tossed.

"Mama, Mommy," David screamed, and Goliath's head turned half-sleepily toward him, his greasy lips greedily catching at the air, a trail of thick saliva trickling down his chin. David stretched the rubber bands and sent the rock out of the sling. "O-o-o-o-o-o-o-o . . ." Goliath yelled. He covered his face with his hands and crashed down. "Mama, Mama. He's dead. I've saved you from Goliath. Let's run, quickly!" Crying and laughing with joy and fear, David shook Mama, dragging her squashed body from under his fallen enemy who was writhing and howling in pain.

Translated by Thomas Epstein and Maxim D. Shrayer

"David and Goliath" (David i Goliaf) was written between 29 June and 1 July 1987 in Ladispoli, a seaside resort outside Rome where David Shrayer-Petrov and his family spent over two months awaiting their American visas. It appeared in the quarterly *Vremia i my* 98 (1987). The present translation was originally published in *Midstream* (February/March 1990).

HURRICANE BOB

Geyer stood at the ocean shore, where the concrete parapet separated the parking lot from the straw-colored sand. It was August. The sun was concluding its arc, moving westward over the very tip of Cape Cod. It was the end of August on the Cape, and the evening was approaching. Fishermen were making their way down to the Atlantic shore that served as a beach during the day and a place for catching bluefish in the evening.

It was August and sunset.

Geyer had come up to Provincetown early that morning. His friend and the friend's wife were expected to join him, driving their own car and bringing a young lady of their acquaintance. About two weeks ago, Geyer and his friend had agreed to meet in Provincetown, to hang around the streets of this exotic place and bask in the sun.

Geyer had been living in America for five years. He had driven up from New Haven where he'd been stuck for two years, draining all the juices from a fellowship that he'd received to finish writing his book, *The French Cottage*. The friend, who lived outside New York City, worked at a pharmaceutical company making antibiotics. Actually, Geyer's friend didn't intend to stay long in Provincetown but planned to continue on to Newport, the final destination of his trip. The meeting in Provincetown was supposed to appear accidental in introducing Geyer to the young lady, who had come from Russia to visit with Geyer's friend and his wife. Geyer knew about these plans from a telephone conversation with his friend, who had spoken in whispers so as not to embarrass the young lady. She happened to be nearby at that moment watching *La Dolce Vita* on video. The upshot was that Geyer and his friend would meet in the center of Provincetown, have a bite to eat, and drive to the beach. And then . . . they would see.

And that's the way it happened. Geyer was the first to arrive; he parked his little Ford on a side street, stopped at a coffee shop, bought a cup to go, and was now standing at the corner of the main promenade and a side street leading to the pier, drinking his coffee and studying the crowd. It was a cheerful crowd. It reminded Geyer of his late-night strolls on the Nevsky Prospekt, in the Leningrad of his youth. Or on Rustaveli Prospekt in Tbilisi, Georgia when he was there investigating the story of *The French Cottage.* This was all back in the '60s and '70s, when he was a young successful science reporter for the leading Soviet periodicals. Long before his attempt at emigration and his voided years as a refusenik . . .

In Provincetown, young men painted like circus clowns were sauntering about, hugging each other. A leggy young woman was pushing a stroller with a baby whose cheeks shone in the sun like anthracite. The young woman was accompanied by a wiry, middle-aged girlfriend dressed in navy uniform. The girlfriend-sailor was smoking a cigarette and humming a bluesy tune in a deep voice. In the coffee shop, Geyer had been served by a man wearing earrings and lipstick. The main street of Provincetown, which ran parallel to the ocean shore, was not very long. Every ten or fifteen minutes, the same parade would pass again by the corner where Geyer stood. The young men decorated like fancy shop windows, the young woman with the baby and the girlfriend in navy uniform, the two old gentlemen in straw hats tied together by a single hatband, a couple of girls showing off French kisses. All this was fun. The scene didn't surprise Geyer or disturb him. It was just another form of American life he had to absorb, without necessarily trying to understand it.

"Geyer, Geyer, here you are, falling right into our hands!" The friend and his wife suddenly emerged from the crowd, shouting and hugging Geyer, kissing him, slapping him on the shoulder, checking out his clothes, exclaiming in *ohs* and *ahs* how wonderful he looks. Geyer's friend contrived to whisper to him, "Look, dude— what an undine!" The undine—that is, the young lady visiting from Russia, who stood waiting to be introduced—could have met all expectations of a promising relationship. She was about ten years younger than Geyer, smiling and slender, with a stylish hairdo, wearing a flowered silk dress, of the sort that hadn't been fashionable in America for some time but gave a gypsy look to a pretty Russian woman. The girl had a warm Russian name that Geyer also liked. When the friend, clandestinely urged by his wife, whispered, "So, what do you think, old man?" Geyer answered quite sincerely, "Great!"

Carried by the crowd, they drifted along the main street. It was their lot to fall into line right behind the stroller with the anthracite baby who had awakened and was now sucking from his bottle. The baby was watched over by two mothers, one of whom was also its father, the sailor. Twice, Geyer and his friends broke away from the promenade: once to buy some lilac-colored shells in a matchbox-size shop, and another time to joke around trying on clothes in an Army-Navy store that sold uniforms and all sorts of junk like compasses, boat steering wheels, sails with skulls and crossbones on them, and copper bells called "hour glasses" on a Russian vessel.

After they'd had enough of sauntering and bumbling in and out of the shops, they decided to find a place to eat. It was getting warm, and the hot asphalt smelled of propane, an odor even stronger than the tang of herring on the ocean breeze. They went to an open-air restaurant with lattice walls and cane furniture, where they chatted about all sorts of amusing and inconsequential things. About Russian restaurants in Brooklyn. About this arrogant man who'd been so busy petting his rust-colored dog that he drove at a snail's pace. So Geyer's friend started a row by honking and flashing his lights behind the slow driver. When the man left his car to have it out with Geyer's friend, the rusty dog jumped onto the highway. The man ran to catch his pet, while Geyer's friend honked a contemptuous *do-re-mi, do-re-do* at him, which to a Russian would have meant *now get lost, you asshole,* and that was the last they saw of him.

Geyer was sitting across from the Russian girl, who talked about how difficult it was to afford an airplane ticket, how long she had saved for it, and how finally she got enough money together, only because she was dying to see America.

Geyer put in a word: "They say that Moscow today is almost like America."

"You mean freedom?" the girl asked.

"Well yes, sure. Because nothing else . . ."

She glanced at Geyer, surprised, but then quickly agreed. "Yes of course, freedom is the most important thing. Especially for people like you. People who had it rough during the period of stagnation."

The friend hurried to call a waiter. They all ordered different salads—chicken, tuna, shrimp, garden. Afterward they lingered over coffee and tarts with strawberry or sour cherry filling. Nothing had clicked yet. Geyer already knew this could only be a trifling relationship at best, leading to nothing but annoyance (for him) and disappointment (for her). However, there was little he could do about it now. He would have to be a gentleman and not let down his well-meaning friends.

It often happened, when Geyer found himself in a hopeless situation of this sort, that he would suddenly discover a hidden door opening to a different plotline. That is, an inspiration would appear out of thin air, and a new adventure would begin. As it was now, with the two women sitting at the next table. One of them Geyer had noticed the moment they entered the restaurant. She was about twenty-three or twenty-five, a beauty who must have stepped down into the room from a Gainsborough canvas—tall, with a long neck, ash-blond hair flying behind her, and celestial blue eyes. Straight out of a classical painting, into this restaurant with brown, entwining shadows, cane chairs, and white-jacketed waiters with sweet voices. She was so quiet and gentle, even in the way she spoke to the waiter. Her girlfriend was also attractive, in a different way. Hers was the elegance of an aristocrat wearing a hunter's outfit, jackboots, and holding a whip in her hand. Only that now, instead of a whip, she held a fountain pen that she was tapping on a typed sheet laid out in front of her on the table. It was obvious that the "Huntress," as Geyer named her, was correcting proofs of something. The Beauty and the Huntress were finishing their lunch very much in the Provincetown spirit of equipolarity: one had tea and cake; the other, Irish coffee.

ଚୟ୍ଥ

Geyer and his friends had a whole day of sunbathing on the beach and swimming in the Atlantic, which was chilly and clear like the waters of a spring. Clear and bitter-salty. From time to time they climbed the wooden stairs and looked out at the whales that seemed to hang motionless on the horizon. The whales spouted tall jets of water that in a strange way reminded Geyer of the fountains of Peterhoff. Although things didn't look too promising for Geyer and the Russian girl, the miracle of sun and sea made him forget the main purpose of coming to Provincetown. They swam and even played together in the water (which raised the hopes of the Russian guest), drank beer, devoured sandwiches, and kicked around a four-colored volleyball. The space their party occupied on the beach was defined on one side by a wet strip of rolling and unrolling waves. Bathers lingered idly on this wet tideline. On the other side, their party's space was limited by groups of Americans who were drying themselves after swimming, sunbathing, eating sandwiches with salami, cheese, and tomato slices, and drinking soda or beer.

From time to time, Geyer would come up with a polite and plausible excuse and leave his companions, making sure that his leaving would not offend them, and his coming back would not reveal any of his disappointment. Actually, he wasn't walking aimlessly back and forth along the water or ironing the sand. He was searching for the Beauty who had stepped down from a Gainsborough canvas. His enthusiasm was fired by an obsessive hope; it simply couldn't happen that the Beauty and the Huntress would vanish from his life, just as easily as they had stepped into it!

"Why don't we start getting back to town?" Geyer suggested, as if incidentally. "It's time to think where we'll be spending the night, my dear ladies and gentlemen!"

They were at the far end of Race Point Beach. The motels and inns were closer to Provincetown, so the others thought Geyer's suggestion to start heading back and looking was reasonable. Besides, everyone was tired from sun and salt water, looking forward to a nice room with a shower in a decent hotel, to supper and an evening stroll that would reveal (especially to Geyer's friends who were in Provincetown for the first time) some exciting scenes. *"Circus naturalis,"* as Geyer's friend called it in his homegrown Russian Latin.

Geyer undertook to be their guide. They drove for a little while along roads flanked by sand dunes sprouting rough grass and desert-like shrubs before they turned onto a main highway lined with hotels and motels on both sides. The girl chose to ride with Geyer; he couldn't very well say "no." Every time they saw a vacancy sign, they would pull over, go in, and talk with the manager. But each time something didn't seem right, and they drove on. Finally, they arrived at a small inn with vacancies right on the waterfront, and they decided to stay there. The women sat on a sofa in the lobby while the men checked in. The friend paid for his room first. When it was Geyer's turn to fill out the form, he asked his friend for the young lady's full name to engage a separate room for her.

"What are you, crazy?" his friend whispered angrily. "Why waste the money?"

"It's better this way," replied Geyer, and he paid for two accommodations.

⟨⟩

It was August, and the setting sun was concluding its arc over the tip of Cape Cod. Geyer stood at the edge of the beach adjoining the inn, right where the concrete parapet separated the parking lot from the straw-colored sand. The rest of his party stayed in their rooms, resting from a day on the beach and getting ready for an evening of entertainment.

Evening life was taking over the beach, different from the daytime when it served sunbathers and swimmers. In the evening the beach belonged to fishermen. They streamed into the parking lot, which was filling up now with their cars as fast as the sun was setting. But it was still bright out, although the sun was no longer warming, only casting light on the shore. Seagulls were landing on the water—a sign, the fishermen said, that an abundant school of bluefish was moving toward shore.

At the far corner of the parking lot, behind a high dune, stood a dilapidated, rust-eaten camper. It looked like a curiosity shop on wheels. The van was crudely decorated with Ukrainian folk ornaments that included some erotic symbols. The back door was ajar, some rollicking dance number rumbling inside, which Geyer immediately recognized as the tune of "Kazachok." That was followed by "Hopak," a Ukrainian dance. Geyer went toward the music.

In the space between the van and the high dune, Geyer discovered a picturesque group of vagabonds. There was a half-naked, hefty man, about fifty years old, longhaired, and made up like a streetwalker. This burly fellow was stepping to the music, keeping time with a ladle in his hand. He was not too busy dancing and conducting to pause briefly and taste the stew simmering in a huge pot hung over a heather-scented open fire. The dancer wore earrings of many-colored glass beads. He was decked out in a necklace of copper and silver coins. His lips were painted the color of rowanberries. His body and right cheek were covered with the half-knitted sores and yellow-pink scabs of healing furuncles. Around the campfire sat a group of his ragged cohorts, differing from each other only by color of skin or hair but not by their tangled hair and dirty clothes. One of them was peeling potatoes, another was cutting into pieces a three-foot striped bass, and a third was opening a gallon of some cheap red wine.

Geyer walked into the camp and greeted the hefty, painted fellow who seemed to be the camp chief. The others paid no attention. Studying Geyer with his shrewd blue eyes, the camp chief welcomed him in Ukrainian, no doubt catching from the guest's accent their common East-Slavic origins. Geyer answered in Russian, "Zdravstvuyte!" ("Hello!"). They began a conversation based on a mixture of Russian, Ukrainian, and English colloquial phrases from a dictionary no one would have the nerve to compile and publish, but whose basic tenets are often pressed into service in similar situations. The big, shirtless fellow who owned the van and the rest of the camp's property was a genuine hobo who lived the free life of the road and music. He constantly cultivated and refreshed his childhood memory of the Ukrainian language and songs, and such a pastime brought him a small profit. Between the sunbathers in the daytime and the fishermen in the evening, there would always be some emigrants from the Russian Empire—tsarist, Communist, or reform-era—who started a conversation with him, requested a par-

ticular song, or even, seeking a taste of exotica, sampled the slop in
the stewpot. Geyer gave a dollar to the camp chief and took off.

Fishermen were strewn from one end of the beach to the other,
each with two or even three fishing rods equipped with Japanese,
Korean, Swedish, or American reels. A fisherman would hold one
of these rods in his hand, propping up the others vertically in plastic
cylinders that were cut at a slant to pierce the sand more easily. Each
one had a tackle box with compartments for hooks, lures, lines,
leaders and other fishing gear.

The evening's fishing was just getting started. The bravest of the
men waded the farthest, the water up to their waist, and cast their
lures about a hundred and fifty feet out to where distant waves
crested in the red rays of the setting sun; from daggerlike splashes the
sparkling bodies of bluefish could only be imagined. Geyer walked
from one fisherman to another, taking heed of different ways of
casting and bringing in the line. After a fight, the long steel-blue
body of the fish would fly out of the water onto the sand, twisting
and desperate to escape when the hook was taken out of its sharp-
toothed jaws. Lucky fishermen would free their lures, stow away
the fish in their bags, and keep fishing. Unlucky ones—the major-
ity—would cast their lures again and again, hoping for a break.

The luckiest was a tall fisherman wearing a striped sailor's shirt,
stylish canvas pants held up by a wide leather belt with a copper
buckle, and rubber waders. He would walk ahead of the others into
deeper water and cast a long green plastic lure with two hooks,
yanking it faster and stronger than the others. He pulled out one
bluefish after another. As they bared their teeth and struck out
fiercely, he stepped on each captive's head and put into its mouth a
metal reamer in order to remove the hooked lure. Immediately, he
would hand out the catch to some nearby spectator, most often one
of the local boys hanging around. As if in a dream, Geyer approached the station of the fortunate fisherman in striped shirt and

waders. Two extra rods stood in white plastic cylinders. An open tackle box, with all the fishing gear, stood on the sand next to a folding chair. It was like being caught in a film, moving from frame to frame—*still, close-up*—in the spell of a director who has ordered the cameraman now to present us with a panorama—*background, moving to foreground*—now to zoom in on the faces, now to focus on the various objects starring in the scene. In just that way, Geyer's gaze was led from an establishing shot of the fishermen standing all along the shore, then to the lucky catcher in his waders, now to the bluefish struggling desperately on the sand, to the smiling, swarthy faces of the boys, to the red box of fishing gear, and then, suddenly—to the Beauty who had stepped out of a Gainsborough canvas and was sitting on a folding beach chair. It was she.

"This guy is incredible," said Geyer to the Beauty, just to say something, rather than staring in silent admiration.

"Yes, Katherine has a brilliant technique," said the Beauty in a deadpan voice. "I'm Pam."

"Geyer," he introduced himself.

As Pam glanced in the direction of the "incredible guy," Geyer understood what an unforgivable mistake he had made. The lucky fisherman was the Huntress who had earlier sat at the table with Gainsborough's Beauty. This revelation made him want to run away, to disappear; he felt so stupid. And how simply all this could have been foreseen! It was Provincetown, after all, Provincetown!

But Geyer couldn't leave as easily as that. First, because his Russian obdurate pride refused to reveal his Russian ignorance, and second, because his Russian daring still nursed a hope in this most hopeless of cases. Given all this, he thought it best to keep the conversation going in a casual, relaxed "on-vacation" manner.

"Are you talking about Katherine's fishing technique? Or the special gear—high-tech rod, super-speed reel, biomagnetic lure?" Geyer forced out a cheerful response, ready to burst out laughing any minute, chasing after Pam's smile. The smile was not meant for him, however, but for Katherine, who had just come up to join them. And what a smile it was—tender, enchanted—the smile of someone who is in love. Geyer's laughter choked off in his throat.

"Would you like to try fishing?" Katherine asked him.

"Yes, very much," answered Geyer. "But I don't have—"

"—no problem!" Katherine cut him short. "You can use this rod. It's lighter. Have you ever fished before?"

"Yeah. But mostly in rivers with a float on the line."

"The time has come to graduate to the ocean," said Katherine, tossing her unfinished cigarette and returning to the waves.

With the borrowed gear, Geyer began casting. He fished for a while, throwing the bluefish behind him in the sand. Later another fisherman who was leaving gave him a sturdy plastic bag for the fish. Far away, as if in a dream, Geyer heard Katherine's voice:

"You can bring the rod to the hotel later. We seem to be neighbors."

He continued to fish, forgetting about everything else in the world. Finally, darkness came. From where Geyer was standing, he could see the vagrants' campfire burning behind the parking lot. He walked over there and handed his catch to the van's owner.

Back at the hotel, under the door to his room, he found a note from his friend: "Hi, old man. We waited for you until eight o'clock. Went out to have supper and walk around." Geyer thought it was all for the best. He wouldn't have to pretend he was an excited but impotent fool in front of the visiting young woman. But he was starved. Geyer went down the road to find some decent place nearby to have a bite. Then he would go back to his room and sleep the night through. Tomorrow he would find a tackle shop, buy his own rod and reel, and fish again—that sweet fishing, a whole evening. Meanwhile, the friend with his wife and the Russian girl would have departed. Geyer would again be free, and alone.

He walked in the direction of the center of town, checking out the restaurants, but none was exactly what he wanted. McDonald's with its tedious hamburgers and wilted salads. Red Lobster, with its fiery sea monsters whose claws threatened to strangle everyone and everything. A Mexican eatery, Tortilla Flats (which Geyer translated into Russian as "Turtle Cave"), with a disgusting blob of brown bean sauce on its sign. As Geyer passed by a Dunkin' Donuts, he looked through the plate-glass window and saw, to his surprise, the Russian girl perched on a high stool. He waved to her but she didn't see him. She was sipping coffee from a styrofoam cup and sobbing. Geyer knocked on the window with his keys. Looking up, she saw him and laughed nervously. When he beckoned to her, she ran out to the street, cup in hand.

"You won't believe how happy I am that you found me, Geyer! I was about to go back to the hotel, and here you are!" said the Russian girl, walking side-by-side with him, still drinking her coffee.

"Wait, wait! How come you're out alone in a strange town at night?" asked Geyer, inwardly cursing the friend, the wife, and himself for this unexpected encounter.

"At first we waited for you. Then we decided to have supper without you," she explained. "We kept searching but still couldn't settle on a suitable place, pleasant yet inexpensive. I realized that, without me, they wouldn't be having this problem. So I said that I was going back to the hotel, I'd had too much sun and wasn't hungry at all."

After she spilled everything to Geyer, she started crying again. She kept crying and repeating that it was her mistake to have made this trip, that nobody wanted her in America, that she should've stayed in her homeland, where she belongs, where her parents and children are. Geyer led her along the street as if she were a blind person, trying to comfort her and saying, again and again, that feeling depressed was typical of those who came from Russia because of the great contrast between the abundance *here* and the poverty *there.* That everything was going to be all right, and that tomorrow they would have a nice day at the beach. They would see the whales on the horizon again, spouting fountains as high as the sky.

They walked amid the evening's carnival crowd; its garish diversity seemed more entertaining than it had in the morning. The young woman told Geyer that she missed her little daughter, who now lived with her grandparents in a *dacha* in the village of Snegiri outside Moscow.

"My father was a colonel in the Air Force; he's been retired now for a long time. And my mother is a housewife." As she continued to tell her story to Geyer, she grew calmer, confiding in him as if he were a trusted intimate.

"And your husband? What's up with him?"

"He exists as a figurehead."

"And in reality?"

"In reality, he and I have come to an impasse. We just can't get around it."

Stopping at the glass door of an upscale Italian restaurant, they studied the pricey, sophisticated menu.

"Shall we go in here?" Geyer offered.

"Oh, no! Why do we need to go to such a restaurant? Look at those prices!" she exclaimed, aghast.

"Don't worry about the prices. Let's just hope the food lives up to them," answered Geyer, feeling that his drive to be alone had only enhanced the memory of Pam's beauty. That his drive to be alone was actually shadowed by an urge to be a hussar on a spree—an urge always lurking within him.

While they were finishing a bottle of Chianti, Katherine and Pam passed by the restaurant window. The girlfriends were chatting, saying words Geyer couldn't hear through the thick glass, but he knew they were happy words. With longing, he watched their bodies, caught in a harmony open only to lovers, disappear from view. Excusing himself to his companion, Geyer ran out into the street. He thought Katherine and Pam were somewhere just up ahead, standing beneath the arch of a big tree, kissing.

Returning to the restaurant, Geyer paid the check, and he and the Russian girl went back to the hotel. He saw her to her room, then retreated to the bar to drink vodka. There was a baseball game on the TV set hanging in the corner of the bar. The bartender reluctantly pulled himself away from the screen to mix vodka with orange juice and ice for Geyer.

"A Tiger Skin," murmured Geyer.

"I beg your pardon?"

"Tiger Skin . . . that's what we used to call this combustible mixture," Geyer explained to the bartender. The bartender polished glasses with a long towel, mixed drinks, and answered something irrelevant to this Russian customer's mutterings. He was barely present in behind the bar, his spirit hovering over the diamond, in a paradise where those darlings of New England, the Red Sox, were playing.

The screwdriver had a calming effect on Geyer, filling in the empty places of his soul the way the tide flows into narrow gullies carved in the sand by its earlier ebbing. He ordered another drink: "Vodka straight!"

"Straight away!" echoed the bartender, pitching a ball in concert with a dazzling baseball hero. "You Russians all drink vodka straight. You may have a mixed drink or two, but then you always switch to straight."

Isn't it funny, thought Geyer, drinking vodka and munching on olives and nuts. Isn't it funny, this bartender's name is Jake. Jacob. Yakov. Yasha. We played *lapta* bat in our courtyard. In '45 or '46, soon after the war. The summer days in Leningrad were long. Only the bat's shadow was short. And the swing had to be short, too.

There was a fat boy, Yasha, who used to come over to Geyer's courtyard. Although he enjoyed watching the boys play *lapta,* he wouldn't play with them—he was afraid. Sometimes the boys missed their target and the bat struck their hands instead of the ball. Or sometimes the heavy ball would hit someone running across the field in the face. Yasha didn't want to risk getting hurt, but he liked to watch them play. The boys used to tease him, wouldn't let him watch, drove him out of the courtyard. Or they missed on purpose, rapping Yasha with the ball while he was sitting under the lilac bushes. He would take off, whining. But burning curiosity always drove Yasha back. Secretly, he would steal back and watch the game out of the window of the washhouse. The one-story brick wash-house had stood there since prerevolutionary times, when the courtyard, Geyer's house, the chapel destroyed in the 1920s by the proletarians, and the grounds had all been part of an almshouse built by its patron, the aristocrat Novoseltsev.

Many years later, Geyer was commissioned by the popular Soviet journal *Hypotheses of the Century* to do a piece about the alterations in salt saturation of the Black Sea and the changes that might be fatal to flora and fauna of the world's oceans, and also about diseases transmitted by the area waterways. On board the steamship *Russia* sailing from Yalta to Sebastopol, after breathing in enough of the sea air and watching the passengers dancing on the open deck, Geyer went down to the bar. There was a TV set in the corner, showing a soccer game between the Zenith and the Torpedo. Being a devoted fan of the Leningrad Zenith, Geyer started talking about the game with a couple of people drinking at the bar and asked the bartender for a shot of vodka.

"Would you like a canapé with some caviar or smoked salmon?" asked the bartender, and suddenly, Geyer recognized in him the fat boy Yasha. They began talking, and Yasha served Geyer drinks on the house.

"You're such a famous journalist. I clip all your articles. Yours and also those about Yurka Dmitriev, from your old building in Leningrad. What a chess genius he is, isn't he! And the way you two used to play *lapta*—it was fantastic!"

"It was fantastic all right, Yasha," Geyer nodded. "We played real tough." It was well past midnight when Geyer got down from the barstool to return to his cabin. The bar was empty.

"Geyer, can I tell you about my dream?" Yashka whispered to Geyer across the counter.

"Go ahead."

"One day I'd like to watch *their* game of *lapta*. A real baseball game. Cruising somewhere on the Atlantic or Pacific. Drinking beer, maybe Heineken, and watching baseball. Remember how much I loved *lapta?*"

"Jake!"

"Yes, sir?"

"One more vodka, straight."

"Okaaaay, sir."

"Also, Jake—you don't happen to have any smoked salmon?"

"Sure thing, sir."

The baseball game ended, and the late night news began. As he listened, without concentrating, to the news anchor's Boston accent, his thoughts drifted to Pam. How beautiful she was. He imagined seeing her on the beach tomorrow and felt a sudden urge to be with her. The news report was about Russia, so Geyer started to pay attention. The president was on vacation in the Crimea. Journalists had been trying unsuccessfully to interview him for days. The bartender brought Geyer a shot of vodka and some lox with a slice of lemon. The lox was yellowish-pinkish and glistened in the semi-darkness of the bar. Now the TV meteorologist was walking beside a map of the United States, among whirlwinds and tornadoes. As he spread his hands, the storms swirled behind his back like pigeons in

Piazza San Marco in Venice. Or in front of St. Isaac's Cathedral in St. Petersburg. Geyer thought for a moment about tomorrow's fishing and listened closer. Several times the meteorologist repeated the words: Hurricane Bob . . . Hurricane Bob . . . Hurricane Bob. In different combinations: Hurricane Bob is approaching Cape Cod from the southeast. Hurricane Bob is packing very strong winds. The area most at risk is Cape Cod, where Hurricane Bob is expected to hit in less than two days.

Great, thought Geyer. I'll still have an entire day at the beach. Although he was not sure which would make him happier—a whole morning of sunbathing and swimming or a whole evening of fishing. Then his friend with the wife arrived, and Geyer treated them to champagne. The Russian girl, seeing no hope in the situation, had earlier retired to her room, but now came downstairs with the friend's wife. And finally, Katherine and Pam, back from their night outing on the town, joined their party. The men, including the bartender Jake, drank vodka, and the women sipped champagne. Geyer remarked that vodka would suit Katherine better—and the lack of political correctness was forgiven him.

Although it was almost midnight and the bar was closed, they stayed there to party. Jake joined them, and they celebrated the Red Sox victory with more drinks. Katherine and Pam tried to convince the Russians to support a platform of sexual tolerance, which would lead to moral entropy. This, they claimed, would result, at last, in world harmony between sexes, races, and nations.

"Let's drink to Campanella," suggested Geyer. They all drank.

"To all those utopias. . . ," Geyer's friend sarcastically remarked.

Katherine ordered champagne in honor of Plato. They drank to Plato. Suddenly the Russian girl cried, "Let's drink to the great poet Tsvetaeva!" They drank to Tsvetaeva. They were all quite drunk at that point.

Jake played a Glenn Miller recording; Geyer's friend and his wife danced under the bar's dimmed lights. Enlivened, the Russian girl invited Katherine—stunning in her navy blue jacket with shining gold buttons—to dance.

Geyer was sitting at the bar next to Pam, who was sipping Veuve Clicquot.

"Pam, since you say you are for entropy," said Geyer, "why don't you run away with me right now?"

"It's very simple, dear Geyer. Because I love Katherine."

"But . . . but does that eliminate any possibility of your loving someone else—man or woman—who would be more dazzling, or let's say, possess the shade of passion that's absolutely perfect for you?"

"Theoretically, it doesn't. But practically, I find it difficult to see someone else in Katherine's place."

Every once in a while, meteorologists, like mute angels, flew across the TV screen. The Russian girl swung rhythmically, clinging to Katherine, who danced with her Habsburg chin resting on her partner's shoulder.

"May we at least dance, Pam . . . please?"

"All right, Geyer, if you insist."

After the dancing, they decided to go for a swim. The ocean licked the sand and their feet like an old loyal dog. In Russia, Geyer and his friends explained to the Americans, it was the custom to top off such an evening by bathing in the nude. Suddenly caught in a moment of indecision, they grew quiet. But one by one, naked, stretched in single file, like kids going skinny-dipping, they ran into the water. Geyer at one end of the line was next to his friend, his friend's wife, and the Russian girl. Pam and then Katherine were at the other end of the line. Dark silhouettes, like bronze sculptures, blended into the waves, then emerged. Geyer couldn't even recognize which one of them was Pam, which his friend, which the Russian girl. "Entropy," Geyer said to himself with a grin, briskly drying himself with a towel.

The Russian couple said good-bye to everyone before going to their room. "Tomorrow we'll visit Newport and then head home to Jersey."

"We should probably go to bed. It's late," said Katherine.

But Pam said, "Geyer, you promised to tell us about your book, *The French Cottage?*"

"I did? Well, I'd be happy to, but where? Isn't it a bit chilly here on the beach? And the bar is definitely closed by now on the occasion of the swiftly approaching hurricane," Geyer tried to sound playful.

"You know what, we could go to my room," said the Russian girl enthusiastically. "Yes! Yes! All of us. I have a special bottle of cherry brandy I brought from Moscow. We'll have a drink, warm up, and Geyer will tell us his French story."

"Great idea!" exclaimed Pam. "Okay, Katherine?"

"Sure, why not? What do you think, Geyer?"

"Sounds good. Who says no to cherry brandy?"

They stayed up until three, drinking the viscous brandy brewed from Ukrainian sour cherries, while Geyer told the story of Georgy Eliava, the young microbiologist from Soviet Georgia, who came to Paris in the 1920s to work with Professor Félix d'Herelle of the Institute Pasteur. How the professor and his disciple had studied the bacteriophage, a virus capable of killing deadly microbes. How these two idealists decided to build in Tbilisi, Georgia, an Institute of Bacteriophage, the first in the world, where they would conduct experiments and clinical trials to save mankind from infections. How they were thrilled after their first few patients were cured, and how Stalin's henchman Lavrenty Beria took his vengeance against them for not cooperating with his own evil plans.

"And then? What became of these romantics?" asked Pam.

"From time immemorial, as you know, history has never dealt *romantically* with its romantics," answered Geyer. "Most often, they have been executed without trials or else were killed in duels. Why is this? Because not only do these romantics and idealists plague the tyrants, they also annoy the common people, distracting them from their meat pots and beer barrels."

After Pam and Katherine left, the Russian girl, whose name was Masha, said, "What a shame that I will never know the end of this French story."

"I will tell you now," said Geyer.

He sat in a wooden chair upholstered in a material so coarse and heavy that it must have been woven back in Pilgrim times. The room was lit by a floor lamp; the straw shade resembled a cartwheel. Masha reclined on her bed, leaning on one elbow, listening.

"The story of the *The French Cottage* comes to an end in 1936. At the beginning of 1936, Professor d'Herelle returns to Paris from Tbilisi, anguished by all sorts of doubts and premonitions. And still, not just because he was an incurable idealist and romantic, but more because he was a great scientist who felt duty-bound to continue this research, he kept waiting for good news from Eliava in Soviet Georgia. A year passed. Not a single letter. It wasn't until late in 1937 when d'Herelle learned that Eliava had been executed by order of Beria. After that, d'Herelle was all alone.

"When the Germans occupied Paris in 1940, d'Herelle was offered work for the army of the Third Reich. He refused to collaborate with the Boches and was imprisoned until the liberation of Paris in 1944. That's it."

Summarizing the events of the story he had spent years researching and turning into a book made Geyer relive it once again. He had grown silent, doleful.

"And you are exactly the same as those two," said Masha.

"What do you mean?"

"Romantic! Fighting for ideals, rushing about from country to country, and so—"

"—and so . . . what?" But Geyer already knew the answer, as he also knew she wouldn't be able to tell him the bitter truth.

"And sew . . . buttons!" She jumped up from the bed and opened the window. In the first light of dawn, on the beach down below the hotel wall, seagulls were marching, picking up bits of crab and shellfish tossed up by the tide. The sun had not yet rolled out of the gray-blue cocktail mixed on the horizon sometime during the night.

"You know what, Masha—write me from Russia, okay?"

"I will. Although our letters don't get through."

"Then call me . . . No, I'll call you myself next week. Or at most, the week after that."

"Of course you will, Geyer, if you don't forget."

Returning to his room, he opened the windows, drew the curtains, and fell asleep to the fretful shrieks of seagulls and the pristine rustle of the ocean. It had been a long time since he had slept so well and for so long. Nothing worried him or pushed him to get up, to write his magazine articles, which had done pretty well for him in America, or his fiction, for which he was having a hard time finding a good publisher. As he slept, Masha and Pam were taking turns in his good dreams. Or they would form a threesome: Geyer, Masha, and Pam, swimming in the night ocean. When they got out of the water, it seemed they were on the beaches of Koktebel in the Crimea, Pärnu in Estonia, or Komarovo on the Gulf of Finland— places so dear to the heart that one loves them even in dreams.

ᕫ

After seeing off his friend, the friend's wife, and Masha, Geyer came to the beach and found Katherine and Pam. Compared to yesterday, the beach looked half-empty. Every now and then, someone mentioned the approaching hurricane. Although people knew the hurricane wouldn't reach the Cape for another twenty-four hours, there was some anxiety in the air. People were even reluctant to swim—they just ducked into the water as if performing a duty, to justify the money that had been spent in coming here and paying for the hotel. And now they would have to wait another whole year for another vacation that could be disrupted as easily as this one by some stupid hurricane named "Bob."

At the beach in her swimsuit, Pam was even more beautiful than yesterday. Her high bust pointed through the elastic fabric of her yellow swimsuit, laced by a thin black belt. Pulled into a pony-tail with a yellow band, her ashen hair revealed a soft neck. When Pam jumped to return the badminton birdie, her blue eyes shone with a mischievous glint, as she cried with each blow, *Unh! Unh!* When she missed, which was often, Katherine would patiently ex-plain a better way to hold the racket and to volley over the net. Katherine's black swimsuit was a jumper, the kind wrestlers wear, designed to show off her bold biceps and the strong muscles of her chest, belly, and thighs.

"A real knight in shining armor," Geyer thought. Using a vari-ation of the same playfully chivalrous tone, he asked permission to drop off his "saddle bags" near them.

"Sure, Geyer, but on condition that you promise to finish the story of *The French Cottage*. Okay?" said Katherine.

"I'm dying to hear it," added Pam.

"Where was is that I left it off?" Geyer asked trying to recollect everything that happened last night.

"You stopped where your protagonist Professor d'Herelle de-cides to return to Paris to finish his projects at the Institute Pasteur, intending to move permanently to the Soviet Union," Katherine spoke. "Then the bar closed, and we all went for a night swim. After that, we drank cherry brandy in your Russian lady friend's room, and you started to tell us about your book. But you didn't finish it. Remember now?"

"Vaguely." Geyer looked at the girlfriends guiltily. "Too much cherry brandy."

Katherine acted as though nothing else was happening, there

was no danger, they should simply relax and be themselves, as they would on any vacation away from their campus routine. But Pam looked nervous. Listening to talk about the hurricane, she made an effort to appear interested, but she wasn't the same—sociable and carefree—as yesterday when Geyer had seen her for the first time. As he stood aimlessly staring at the dark ocean, Katherine reminded him again of his promise to finish telling the story of *The French Cottage*—only to forget about it five minutes later as she, too, grew uneasy, watching the beach become more and more deserted. Pam was trying to lose herself in her knitting while the people streamed out of the beach like sand falling through an hourglass.

"Say, Pam, should we pack now, perhaps have a bite to eat, and start driving toward the mainland—before it gets too trafficky?" Katherine finally said, trying to sound nonchalant.

"Yes, I think we should," Pam replied slowly, her voice muffled. She didn't look at Katherine or Geyer but surveyed the ocean and the deserted beach. "What are you going to do, Geyer?" she asked.

"I'm staying. I'll buy myself a rod and reel and try to fish this evening," he answered with such jaunty bravado that both women burst out laughing and kept chuckling and teasing each other— "Well, aren't you so prudent? Aren't you so cautious?"—while they packed their beach bag.

"Good-bye, Geyer. Don't stay here too long," said Pam, kissing him on the cheek.

"If you happen to be in our neck of the woods, please call on us," Katherine said, and shook his hand firmly. "It would be a good opportunity to finish telling your story."

At first he didn't understand which story—the story of his life, of *The French Cottage,* or of what happened to him when Hurricane Bob came to town. So he didn't reply. Katherine understood his silence and didn't try to clear it up. From the parapet, she yelled: "I'll leave our phone number for you. And also a rod and some gear. Good luck fishing!"

掔

The receptionist gave Geyer a look that meant, "Are you crazy?" The hotel had been deserted since lunchtime. Only this Russian wouldn't check out and was even going fishing, judging by the rod he was carrying. This crazy Russian and also Jake the bartender, who bragged that he would have a scotch with Bob.

Seagulls flooded the evening beach. Geyer went back to the place where he had caught bluefish yesterday, not far from where Katherine had been fishing. Before he got ready to cast, Geyer looked back. In the farthest corner of the parking lot, at the bottom of a high dune, stood the same dilapidated, rusted camper, crudely painted with Ukrainian ornaments and erotic signs and symbols. Just as the day before yesterday, the back door was ajar and smoke was winding over the hobos' camp. Nothing in the world seemed more desirable to Geyer at this moment than to catch some bluefish and bring the catch over to the fellow with the painted face, to have supper by the campfire, whiling away a lonely evening.

He was alone on the shore except for a few fishermen—the local Portuguese men—and some indefatigable boys chasing a ball along the empty beach. Dashing up to anyone taking a bluefish off the hook, one of the boys would sometimes be rewarded with a bluefish. Fishing was so great that Geyer once again stayed on the beach well into the twilight, when he had to cast into the distance by relying on what his muscles had learned during the earlier hours of fishing. He cast out the lure and immediately began to reel it back out of the dark purple water. Bringing in the lure, he would push the rod up and down to tease the bluefish. He couldn't see much, but could feel the strike of the fish attacking it. The strike was a signal to yank the rod up abruptly, and also the start of a new wave of joyous excitement—the fight—rolling over him, following earlier waves of delight.

He didn't have a flashlight. It became so dark that it was impossible to cast the reel or take the fish off the hook. The Portuguese fishermen left with their catch. The boys ran home. Seagulls flew away. At the far end of the beach, the campfire was still burning.

"Here I am, and with another catch," said Geyer to the owner of the van, who was smoking a stogie that emitted a pungent scent, sipping tea from a ceramic mug, and watching a portable TV set.

They were showing the progress of the hurricane from North Carolina up along the coast toward New England. Behind the meteorologist's back, whirlwinds were bustling all over the map. With the volume turned up high, the meteorologist now looked rather like the Angel of Death Azrael prophesying a catastrophe. At first, neither the chief nor any of his friends paid any attention to Geyer and his catch. They were busy discussing their itinerary, planning to take off at dawn at the latest and, having had their supper, were getting ready to go to sleep.

"Hey, it's you, Mr. Goodman! And you thought of treating us to some fish!" the chief finally said to Geyer.

"Here—I brought my catch, but it looks like I'm too late. You've already finished supper," muttered Geyer, showing his plastic bag of fish and nervously knocking his rod on the concrete of the parking lot.

"You can't get too much of a good thing," answered the chief. He turned to the other hobos, whose faces were lit by the fire in a way that made it impossible to tell if they were male or female, black or white. "Isn't that true, fellas?"

"Yeah, but if we're going to start cooking again, we'll need something strong to drink. The nights are getting cold," said a man of about thirty with a shaved head who was stretched out on his mat. The other one was either too lazy or detested Geyer so much that even the lure of a drink couldn't get him to respond.

"Yeah, a shot of pepper vodka with fried fish would be nice," the chief said pensively.

"A shot of pepper vodka," echoed Geyer. Suddenly he craved a drink of this fiery liquid, that would wash away the memory of the useless encounters and meaningless conversations of the last two days. "But where on earth can we get pepper vodka at this time, my friend?"

"As the story goes, if you sweep the barn floor and pry into the nooks and crannies, a bottle of pepper vodka may turn up somewhere!" answered the chief, ordering one of this cohorts to stir up the fire and the other one—the guy with the shaved head—to clean Geyer's bluefish.

"Seek out this secret bottle, my friend. I'll pay!" said Geyer, digging in his pockets so energetically that the chief did not hesitate to dive into his van and bring back a bottle of Ukrainian pepper vodka, its label picturing a fiery red comb of hot pepper.

While the fish were frying, Geyer went back to the ocean. Unusually heavy waves rolled onto the shore, bringing with them sounds of crashing and cracking, as if some giant eagles had swooped down from tops of pines and were alarming the night with desperate screeching and flapping of wings. He felt overwhelmed by a dogged despair. The day's fishing had ended, and night brought with it the realization of his loneliness. Returning to the scene of yesterday's skinny-dipping, he watched the waves roll in. They seemed to be swimmers' bodies coming closer, then receding into infinity. He thought he heard their voices: Pam's easy, varied cadence along with the low, sad tone of Masha's. It was time to go back to the camp.

The chief called from the parapet. "Hey, Mr. Goodman! The fish are ready!"

Geyer returned to the campfire. A cast iron pan with fried fish was sitting on a wooden crate. A glossy cover of *Life* magazine served as a dish for thick slices of tomatoes and cucumbers next to cloves of garlic and sprigs of parsley. There were two folding stools, one on each side of the box.

"Where are the others?" asked Geyer, pointing to the stools but meaning the other hobos.

"They've had their share. Full and drunk," explained the chief, whose name was Pete. "People should be fed but not coddled. Each one should be kept in his place."

I can't believe they have the same old saw here: each one should be kept in his place, Geyer thought grimly. Suddenly, he no longer wanted to drink with the chief—but he couldn't just take off. Pete poured pepper vodka into two small, faceted glasses. "Cheers!" They drank up and ate the fish and vegetables. Waves were raging against the shore. The TV kept repeating, "Hurricane Bob . . . Bob . . . Bob." Possible damage was estimated. People were advised to evacuate homes in the flood area. Geyer listened to his host's story while thinking of something else. First the Germans had horded Pete's parents away, but after the war they managed to get to Canada where they had relatives. They bought a farm and settled down, but Pete didn't inherit the love of farming. Nor did he take to heart their nostalgia for Ukraine. He had no desire to visit the ancestral home and search out his roots in a peasant hut.

"I don't want that farm in Canada, nor that old house in the Poltava region. I only care about my freedom. That's why I'm a wanderer. Let's drink to freedom, Mr. Goodman!"

And I'm exactly the same, just like this hobo, thought Geyer. Nothing is as dear to me as freedom. "Yes, to freedom!" They stayed up a while. Then the fire went out. It became chilly, and the vodka bottle was empty. It was time to go back to the hotel and sleep.

"You're welcome to stay here, Mr. Goodman. We'll warm each

other up in the van." The chief burst out with laughter so resounding that his bracelets and earrings jingled like cymbals.

"You son of a bitch!" Geyer whispered under his breath, but he said a respectful good-bye and headed up to the hotel.

淀

The wild roaring of ocean and wind and the crashing of waves against the parapet woke him up. The clock read twelve noon. How Geyer could have slept in the midst of this hell was beyond comprehension. He moved aside the corner of the heavy blind and saw a gray mass of water, sand, wind, and rock that was rolling against the shore with the stubborn insistence of antediluvian Titans rebelling against world harmony. He felt hungry, but first he wanted to know what was going on with the weather. He went down to the lobby; there was no one at the desk.

"Anybody here?" Geyer called loudly. No one responded. Seeing that the door was open, he went down a few steps to the bar and saw Jake holding a drink and watching TV. The screen showed a city at night, fires blazing, and people carrying beams, boxes, crates, and bricks to build barricades. An evil premonition struck Geyer's heart. "Jake, what's going on?"

Without saying anything, the bartender poured Geyer a vodka and waited for him to down it. Sipping from his own glass, Jake said, "We got Hurricane Bob . . . and you guys got a coup."

"God, no! I don't believe it. This cannot be," Geyer cried out with such despair that Jake poured him another vodka and took a long sip from his own glass. Jake waited for the Russian to wash down his vodka with some club soda, then started to make coffee.

Every half hour the TV segments changed. Here in New England—ominous darkness, enraged ocean, a shoreline helpless against the elements, rescue teams at work. There in Moscow—barricades, night fires, desperate people determined to defend their freedom, and tanks sent out to crush them.

While Geyer sipped coffee and ate a sandwich Jake had whipped up for him, the screen continued to alternate pictures of New England and Moscow. Geyer kept repeating over and over again, "A nightmare. Is this the end?" He reverted to Russian, sometimes speaking the words only in his mind, so Jake saw only tears in the eyes of his strange guest who didn't want to escape the hurricane. These crazy Russian heroes, Jake thought, meaning both Geyer and those who stood at the barricades, defying tanks. Yesterday he had been annoyed with this guest, the only one unwilling to check out and leave. The guest had returned to the hotel last night, after both the manager and the receptionist had decamped, leaving the whole responsibility for the hotel on the bartender's shoulders. At first Jake had been angry, but now he thought it was all for the best. The hurricane would dissipate, the bar would be kept intact, and the credit would go to him. In these circumstances, there was always a chance of robbery and looting. There were plenty of thieves around! So by the time Geyer showed up in the bar, Jake was no longer cross with this Russian; instead he felt sympathy for him.

The bar was located below the level of the lobby and had no windows, and the sound of the elements did not reach down there. Geyer couldn't have said how long he stayed in the bar. On the screen he saw pictures of the Atlantic shore ravaged by the hurricane and shots of the city gnashing its teeth at the barricades. He drank vodka or coffee and told Jake the story of his life in the country that was on the verge of catastrophe again. Jake, in turn, told Geyer the story of his own life in the country where Hurricane Bob was smashing the coastline. Jake had a fiancée who lived in Warwick, Rhode Island. She worked as a receptionist in a dentist's office and usually came up to Provincetown to see Jake on the weekends. She would spend the day at the beach, and at night, after the bar closed, they would make love.

"Look, sir, what the hell would she be doing here in this weather?"

Geyer agreed that there was nothing for Jake's fiancée to be doing here this weekend.

"And why should I go down there? A bartender never quits his post. Even if you had checked out, sir, and the hotel had been completely empty, how could I run out on the business even for one day?"

Geyer agreed that a real business could not be abandoned even for one day.

"And if that's the case, sir, how could your leader there, the one who's been changing and reforming everything—how could he abandon his country in such a dangerous moment and go for a vacation in the Crimea?"

"Terrible mistake," answered Geyer.

"If I know there's a good chance that the hotel property would be looted when there's a disaster like this hurricane, how can I take a break?"

"No, you can't, Jake," answered Geyer.

"So what your top guy did was worse than a terrible mistake, wouldn't you say, sir?"

"Far worse," agreed Geyer.

They had another drink, having reached agreement about both countries. Then the meteorologist on the screen said that the hurricane appeared to be turning away from New England and heading out to sea.

A man with a grave face and tired blue eyes came out to join the people on the barricades. He began to speak about the unbearable price of losing their new freedom. As he spoke, he faced the tanks' guns targeted at the barricades, and he kept on speaking until the tanks started to turn back and leave Moscow.

ᏧᎳᏫᎤ

Geyer and Jake sat awhile drinking and talking about life. Then Geyer went back to his room and fell asleep. The next morning, when he came out of the hotel, he found the shore turned upside-down, strewn with rocks, thick lumps of seaweed, and boat wreck-age. The seagulls were still in hiding, God knows where. Geyer went toward the parking lot, where Pete's camper had been parked at the far end. The hurricane had washed away the coals and ashes of the fire. As if nothing had ever been there, Geyer thought. Somewhere, on the far horizon of his memory, stood the figures of Pam and Masha. Not even figures—shadows, rather—dim recollections of happenings from a time long ago. He returned to the hotel and went down for the bar.

Jake, cheerful and clean-shaven, was drying glasses.

"Some coffee this morning, sir?"

"That would be great, Jake." Geyer sat at the bar in front of Jake and began to drink his coffee. On screen, Newport Harbor came into view. Yachts had been crushed like eggshells. Cameras scanned the faces of people as they came upon their wrecked yachts. The people were crying. Then the scene shifted to Moscow. An Orthodox priest and a rabbi were reading the burial service for those who had been killed at the barricades.

"Let's have a drink, Jake," said Geyer.

"Okaaay, sir!"

Translated by Dolores Riccio and Emilia Shrayer

"Hurricane Bob" (Uragan Bob) was composed between April and May 1994 in Providence, Rhode Island. It was published in Russian in the émigré annual review *Poberezh'e* 5 (1996). The results of the author's research on the life and work of Felix d'Herelle in Soviet Georgia appeared in a condensed form as: D. P. Shrayer, "Felix d'Herelle in Russia," *Bulletin de l'Institut Pasteur* 94 (1996): 91–96. The present translation appears for the first time.

HÄNDE HOCH!

We were visiting the Wassers in Athol, a small town in rural north-central Massachusetts. We had met the Wassers—Ernest and Judith—during a trip to Spain. On the first day of the tour their seats happened to be next to ours on the bus. We hit it off with them, so for the rest of the trip we sat together, chatting. We talked a lot about Russia. They asked many questions. We reminisced. The Wassers turned out to be great admirers of Jewish memoir literature. Both of them loved to read reminiscences of Jewish writers, philosophers, and scientists. Even recollections of those from the inner circle of our people's greats fascinated the Wassers. And in the highest esteem they held accounts by survivors of Nazi concentration camps. After we told them that Mila (my wife) and I had waited for almost nine years to emigrate, that is, had been refuseniks during those years, the number of their questions about living in Russia rose so dramatically that we could no longer concentrate on the tour guide's explanations. We could only follow with our eyes along the hills on which olive trees stood like chess pieces. Or else we could guess, from the silhouettes of windmills, that the melancholy knight Don Quixote had galloped across these valleys and mountain passes. Of course, Don Quixote had inherited his eternal sadness from the Jews of Spain.

I've observed that American Jews like to talk about Russia. This is especially true of the ones whose ancestors came from Eastern

Europe. They often speak of it with such excitement and enthusiasm as if Russia, and not Israel, was their forefathers' ancient homeland. But the Wassers truly shared a connection to the vast expanse of fields and great forests, where Mila and I had been born and lived until the late 1980s. As children, both of the Wassers were taken to Siberia. In 1939 their parents, Polish Jews from Lublin, had miraculously escaped from the Nazis and fled to the Soviet Union. Together their families had lived through evacuation to Siberia. Together they returned to Poland after the war, only to flee again, this time to America. The rescuing hand belonged to a Jew from their old neighborhood in Lublin who had settled in the American town of Athol, Massachusetts, a few years before the outbreak of the war. He was searching for his relatives in Lublin. All of them had been killed, and the letter was forwarded to the Wassers, Ernest's parents. Because Judith's parents, the Zolotowskis, were their only friends and fellow survivors, both families replied with one letter, composed in the Aesopian language of hints and allusions. But their fellow countrymen were able to figure it out, and the new American from Athol sent both families an invitation with an affidavit, recognizing them as blood relatives. Ernest and Judith—now the American teenagers "Ernie" and "Judy"—went to school in the small New England town.

Ernie became a salesman in the furniture showroom his father had opened. Judy worked in a bakery. They got married. Judy stayed home with the children. By the time we met the Wassers in Spain, Ernie had retired, leaving the business to his son. Their daughter was living in Providence, Rhode Island, with her husband, a professor of sociology at Brown, and a five-year-old son . . .

ᏬᎥᎥᎥᎽᎧ

"Tomorrow you'll meet the whole *mishpoheh*," Ernie promised me on the phone. "Do you know how to get here? And I want you and Mila to come early. We'll have an unrushed dinner, talk a while. You know how your pockets are always full of interesting news about Russia. Remember, in the evening we're all going to shul to see a play?"

How could I forget?! Ernie was talking about a play that was being put on by the Jewish Theatrical Society. The Jewish Theatrical Society of Athol was well known in the area for its productions of plays translated from the Yiddish. They also staged plays based on the works of Jewish fiction writers, Sholom Aleichem, Isaac Bashevis Singer, and others. Along with the invitation to attend the opening performance I had received a letter from the local rabbi (also the director of the play). The rabbi-director wrote that if the nature and style of the production appealed to me, they would commission from me a play based on my novel about refuseniks, *Herbert and Nelly.* Writing a play based on my own novel—what could be better!

Early spring. The beginning of April. A Massachusetts of fir trees. We drive north, then west, then turn north again. The woods become denser and dimmer. Dark wet branches of the firs reach down to the pink-and-gray granite clefts. The roads here are winding and narrow, slithering along like black asphalt snakes. By five o'clock our Subaru swallows the last twists and turns of the road, and we're in Athol.

We drive up the main street past the gray ferroconcrete building of the bank, a red brick fire station, and a lemon-colored hotel with false columns and a bright white trim. The town's only stoplight winks at us: here we turn right. We cross a bridge over an uproarious stream. The red neon sign of the local paper, the *Athol Times,* is also in the directions Ernie Wasser gave me over the phone. And here's the final landmark: a painted sign of a furniture store and a section of a bedroom in the store window. Two more minutes, and we turn into the Wassers' long driveway.

Their house is a large Victorian with a wraparound porch. Or-
nate cast iron railings. Cast iron grates on the first floor windows. A
solid, stately house where the Wassers have been living since the
1950s. The house is flanked on one side by an apple orchard. Lilac
trees mark off the boundaries of the property on the other side.
Rhododendrons are planted in the front; they are swollen, ready to
burst into bloom. A Teutonic-looking giant strolls in the garden
with a boy of five or six. The boy is clutching a baseball bat in his
right hand. The giant turns out to be Wilhelm (Willy), the Wassers'
son-in-law, and the quick-eyed and mischievous boy is his son
Mark, their grandson.

We learn all this immediately after parking our Subaru near the
gates of the carriage house now used as a garage. We park our car,
remove our weekend bag from the trunk, and fall into the hands of
Ernie Wasser, kissing and hugging him, petting King the chocolate
spaniel on his fluffy ears, being introduced to Willy, little Mark and
also to Jessica, the Wassers' daughter. Our arrival has inadvertently
distracted Willy and Mark from an important activity. The giant
apologizes and leads Mark away into the far corner of the garden,
from where we soon hear guttural sounds of foreign speech.

"Our son-in-law is teaching our grandson German," Ernie explains, and takes us inside to say hello to Judy, who is in the kitchen.
We go up to the guest room to drop our bag. Mila hurries back
down to help Judy and Jessica. I linger in the room, examining a
pyramid of books on the nightstand between the two twin beds.
Many of the books are on Jewish history: Jews in Morocco, the Inquisition, the destiny of Poland's Jews. I leaf through a book of photographs from Auschwitz: stacks of corpses, smoking chimneys,
piles of footwear that belonged to the people gassed alive . . .

The ellipsoidal table is set for eight: the Wassers (Ernie and
Judy), the Hoffmanns (Willy, Jessica, and Mark), Mila and myself,
and also another gentleman whom Ernie introduces to us as a "very

dear guest." While making the introductions, Ernie gently nods, licks his dry lips and timidly smiles. I know his mannerisms, the timid smile that accompanies the welling up of tears in his eyes.

"A very dear guest. A special guest," Ernie repeats. The Wassers' special guest sits across from me. His name is Jan Silberstadt. He is well over eighty. The coat of his black two-piece suit hangs on the back of his chair. He is silent, concentrating on the meal.

We're served a standard Jewish-American dinner: lettuce dressed with oil and vinegar; chicken broth with egg noodles; roast chicken with white rice and carrots, and prune compote. The traditional Jewish compote! My grandmother Freyda used to make it every week: prunes plump like Odessan women, water, sugar, and a drop of starch for thickness. Sweet with a barely tangible bitterness, like a Jewish wedding song. And a freshly baked *babka* with raspberry jam. A bottle of Shiraz stands in the middle of the table. At the beginning of the dinner Ernie offers everyone some wine; only Mila and I accept.

"Is there any vodka?" Willy asks loudly.

The master of the house nervously licks his lips and removes a bottle of Stoli from a glass cabinet. The bottle is nearly full. Mila and I each drink a glass of wine. Willy downs two shots of vodka in a row. "Russian vodka is very good!" he says and smiles at us. The elderly guest lowers his gaze into the bowl of chicken broth with noodles. Ernie stops offering drinks. He even puts the wine and vodka away into the glass cabinet. However tempting, it would be *inaccurate* to attribute to inebriation a certain argumentative brashness that both Mila and Willy show during the dinner, since neither one of them has had much to drink. Inaccurate versus accurate . . . the English language here displays a proclivity to evaluate the method employed in the presentation of a given piece of information. The English language assesses the method rather than the underlying ethic, as would my native Russian language, in which I would be inclined to say *dishonest* instead of *inaccurate*. Dishonest versus honest . . .

For some reason the dinner conversation turns to the subject of automobile license plates.

"In many European countries, including Russia, things are much easier," Mila says. "License plates tell you in which city or which county center the car is registered. Someplace in Belgium, at a gas station or in a hotel parking lot, you see a car whose license plates say it's from Amsterdam. And you just happen to be driving to Amsterdam from Paris. So you strike up a conversation with the owner of the car. You find out something that you cannot extract from any guidebook."

"But not everyone wishes to inform the whole world where he or she lives," Willy retorts. "I prefer the American system with the name of the state and a combination of numbers and letters on the license plates."

"What's to hide? Amsterdam, St. Petersburg, Venice! The names alone possess their own charm, their flavor and color. They evoke so much—the lace of canals, the necklaces of bridges. It's not like it says Dachau on the plate!"

Ernie drops his fork. It's good that the average American doesn't use both knife and fork simultaneously. Otherwise it would have sounded like the entrance of the percussion instruments at the culmination of an orchestral piece. I mean, if you take a dinner conversation to be a symphony with its adagio, its andante, and its strong finale with a crescendo. Ernie picks up his fork and puts in his lap his grandson Mark, who is happily consuming chicken with rice. They say the protective centers of the brains of children and animals are much more sensitive as compared to adult humans.

"So what, so what about Dachau?" Willy attacks my wife. "Say, I was born in Dachau. And if I continued to live there, and not in this country, the license plate on my Volkswagen would reveal the name 'Dachau.'"

Ernie looks guiltily at his special guest Jan Silberstadt, who continues to eat, unperturbed by the agitation. I try to calm Mila, stroking her right hand, in which she holds an old silver-plated knife. Sometimes it helps, but not now. Mila pays no attention to my preemptive patting of her hand. Her gray-blue eyes turn the steely color of a thunderous sky.

"If I had the misfortune of being born in Dachau," she burst out, "I would run as far as I can from there at the first opportunity. Which, I suppose, you did."

"My husband didn't need to run from any place or to any place. Wilhelm was invited to Brown University because of his world-renowned research on the social psychology of populations living near sites of massive executions," Jessica weighs in. Everything about her is impressive: head, bosom, hips.

Willy takes over from his wife after biting into and swallowing some chicken from a drumstick. "I was able to discover many similarities among the Poles, Germans, and Latvians residing in the vicinities of Oswięcim, Dachau, Salaspils, and other place bearing the burden of sorrowful memories."

"A sense of shame?" Mila asks, to clarify his point.

"Actually, more of a sense of bitterness," the Brown professor replies.

"And I would die of shame at the mere thought that I'm a native of Dachau!" Mila shakes my calming hand off of hers. That's what she's like in wrath, my darling lifelong companion.

"And what about the natives of Vinnitsa, in Ukraine, where officers of the NKVD shot thousands of their fellow citizens right within the boundaries of the city? Or the residents of Petersburg with their infamous 'Big House'? Or take the Muscovites with their Lubyanka? You're from Moscow, aren't you? Weren't you ashamed to shop at Detsky Mir, the 'Children's World' department store in Dzerzhinsky Square? It stands right next to the KBG headquarters in whose underground cells they interrogated, even in your times, yes, interrogated the dissidents and Jewish refuseniks? No, I believe the only acceptable responses to such situations are bitterness, sorrow, and deep regret that such evil crimes have been committed," says Willy and sighs, looking over his shoulder at the glass cabinet where Ernie stored away the alcohol. What's there to say? This professor is no dummy.

Throughout the entire discussion the Wassers' special guest Jan Silberstadt hasn't uttered a single word . . .

The synagogue is filled with congregants and their guests. It was only built a year ago. Inside the smell of fresh varnish on the rafters and woodwork is laced with the aroma of freshly brewed coffee. Along the walls, narrow tables stand heavy with coffee thermoses and trays with the uncomplicated New England desserts: cookies, brownies, apple pies. From a distance, platters of fruit resemble exotic oriental ornaments. Each family has contributed something.

The Jews of Athol are dressed in their best clothes. Men wear suits (many of them three-piece). A number of women wear heavy long dresses with sequins. Necklaces and bracelets; costume jewelry, gold, precious stones. The congregants are excited to attend the new production at their shul. But they also pay handsome tribute to the coffee and desserts, each of which follows its own family recipe. The people stand near the long tables or mill around, saying hello to each other. Children snatch away pieces of desert and cavort around the hall. They don't care about the play. Their peers and the holiday atmosphere is enough entertainment for them.

From time to time we can see through the doors of the main sanctuary a costumed actress or actor sticking their heads through a chink in the middle of the curtain and smiling at someone in the audience. Besides the Wassers, we don't know a single soul in Athol. We're being introduced left and right. Some people have heard about my refusenik novel, most likely from the Wassers. Many here are concerned about the future of the Jews still living in Russia. We can see it in the way they speak to us. We're touched. We're grateful to the Wassers for their invitation.

The people are filling the sanctuary and sitting down. A crowd's hum metamorphoses into whispering. Everyone awaits the beginning of the play. The curtain heaves like a sail caressed by gentle breeze. Now and then a baby's crying interrupts the quiet that precedes the miracle of a performance. Finally the rabbi–director comes on stage. He describes the play which the members of the Jewish Theatrical Society are about to perform. The play is based on a memoir by Jan Silberstadt, a former inmate of Dachau. The director explains that his play faithfully follows the events of the love story that Jan Silberstadt describes in his memoir. Everything has been preserved: the real names and even the turn of the plot that brings about the final scene. The director comes down from the stage and approaches the front row. We're all sitting in the same row with Jan: Ernie, Judy, Mila, and I, Willy with Mark in his lap, and Jessica. The rabbi shakes the hand of the Wassers' solemn guest and asks him to stand on stage. The Athol community greets the survivor with big applause. The play begins.

The set depicts a Jewish ghetto in a Polish city occupied by the Nazis. A stone archway; an overgrown courtyard with a desolate chestnut tree; a room with an old upright piano. This is the meeting place of the ill-fated young lovers, Anka and Jan. The Nazi administration has announced, through the local Judendrat, the upcoming deportations of the ghetto residents. From books and films about the Holocaust, the audience knows that "deportation" means transport to concentration camps where the Jews (mothers, wives, daughters separated from fathers, husbands, brothers) will be gassed alive and then burned in crematoria. Reminded of the horrors, the audience expects a tragic ending of the love story. Start the final scene.

Anka's room. Outside the windows—whistles of policemen,

barking of guard dogs, shooting. Anka is behind the piano. Jan sits beside her with his cello. They play Mendelssohn's "Song Without Words." Banging of fists and clattering of heavy boots resound across the room. Anka and Jan continue playing. Nazi soldiers break the door. Their machine guns are aimed at Anka and Jan. The soldiers yell: "Hände hoch! Hände hoch!" The piano gives out a plaintive sound. The cello drops to the floor. The curtain falls. A screen descends from the ceiling. Rays of the slide projector bring to the screen brick chimneys of the crematoria. Heavy smoke. The camp's gates. A solitary figure of an inmate in a striped uniform. Chimneys. Smoke. Smoke. Smoke. The screen is pulled up. Lights go out, and the curtain is raised again. Everyone applauds the actors, the director, the Wassers' guest Jan Silberstadt.

To preserve the fullness of all the events, I should add that when the Nazi soldiers broke into Anka's room and rabidly shouted: "Hände hoch! Hände hoch!," many in the audience were shaken. The tragedy of European Jewry came alive before their eyes. At that point Willy whispered "Excuse me" and left to put Mark to bed. Jessica followed them.

The success of the play has exceeded all expectations. Actors and actresses, especially the two who played the lead parts of Anka and Jan, are surrounded by relatives and friends. In Athol all the Jews are friends or relatives, usually both. The members of the audience come up to congratulate the cast and director, discuss the most memorable episodes, ask the director when he plans to start working on the next production.

Old Jan Silberstadt looks tired, spent. At first the people approach him with questions: "Where can we buy or order your memoir? How close is the play to real life? What are you working on now?" He replies reluctantly, dryly, disallowing any hearty conversation. They finally leave him alone.

The thespian rabbi now takes me to his study in the opposite end of the synagogue. The walls are adorned with works of Israeli artists, including David Sharir.

"I love his work!" the rabbi exclaims. "He lives in Tel Aviv."

"Yes, I know his paintings very well," I reply. "He's my cousin."

"By the way, what did you think of the production?" asks the rabbi.

"Excellent set, very good directing, fine acting," I answer. "Very professional."

"Do you have anyone in mind we could commission to do the sets for your play?"

"I would recommend Boris Sheynes. He's a former refusenik. Knows the specifics of the period."

"Excellent! Excellent! You're the author, you know what's best," the director replies.

We discuss the terms: number of characters, deadline for the play, honorarium. Then the rabbi walks me back to the sanctuary, now empty except for Ernie, Judy, Jan, and Mila who are all waiting for me. We drive back to the Wassers' house . . .

Neither of us can fall asleep. We turn on the TV. Scraps of thrillers, hackneyed game shows, beauty pageants don't help chase away the burdensome thoughts. What's changed? Hundreds of thousands tortured or expelled by the Inquisition. Six million turned to tears and ashes by the Nazis. Tens of thousands herded by the Soviets into the ghettos of refusenik isolation and persecution. And once again, just a few weeks ago, in California: burned synagogues and murdered children. When will this stop? Will it ever?

Mila and I discuss the play. We both wonder if the performers, the director, the set designer have been completely successful in preserving the character of Silberstadt's memoir.

"You know, the final scene, the very last episode, did you think it was a bit too simplistic, with the soldiers shouting their 'Hände hoch!'? A little formulaic, like those Soviet war movies?" Mila asks me.

I hesitate to respond. I also think that something in the final episode was off. Had it really happened like this? And even if it had, should a reflection of the past be a mere copy of the original? And the most important: do I want now, many years hence, to see the things we lived through as refuseniks with the same eyes in my future play as I did in my novel? I want to say all this to my wife, but she's already fallen asleep.

I go downstairs and find Willy in the dining room; a bottle of vodka stands in front of him on the table.

"Would you like some Stoli?" he asks.

We have a drink together and talk about the weather. It turns out Willy is a passionate fisherman, just like me. He keeps a motorboat down in Narragansett Bay. We discuss the weather, fishing, his preference of Stoli over Smirnoff and my preference of Absolut over Stoli. We have another drink and chat, chat, chat about the weather, fishing, Stoli, Smirnoff, Absolut . . . About anything under the sun, anything except the play. It's getting late, I get up to go to bed.

"Did you like the performance?" Willy asks and looks at me, expecting an answer.

"On the whole, yes," I answer. "Good night." I don't want to discuss it with him.

"In reality, everything was just like that—," Willy's words catch up with me on the stairs, "—and wasn't."

Next morning Mila wakes me up. "Wake up, sleepyhead! We'll take a walk before breakfast. Don't you want to see the town?"

We go out to the front porch. It has rained overnight. Shiny drops hang on the white and amethyst clusters of lilacs. A large blue-winged bird swings on a long fir branch, getting ready to continue on his journey. Where to? Old Jan Silberstadt sits on a cast iron bench near the porch, reading the Sunday paper. We go up to him to say hello.

"There you go, look: Germans protecting Albanians from Serbs. The world is going mad!" says the old man and shows us a photo from the newspaper. Burly lads in military uniform and helmets ride on tanks into Kosovo.

Before we've had a chance to reply to him, we see Willy running out of the apple orchard and onto the front lawn. He is laughing as he raises his arms and bends the elbows. Armed with a toy machine gun, little Mark chases him across the lawn. Ecstatic, the boy doesn't even notice us. Laughing the happiest of laughs, he pursues the giant Willy. At the top of his lungs Mark screams: "Surrender, daddy! Please surrender, daddy! Hände hoch! Hände hoch! Hände hoch!"

Translated by Maxim D. Shrayer

Written in Providence, Rhode Island, in 1999, the Russian text of "Hände Hoch!" bears the same title, a German phrase that means "hands up." It originally appeared in *Forverts* (14–20 January 2000). The Moscow-based monthly *Nasha ulitsa* (Our street) reprinted "Hände Hoch!" along with two other stories by David Shrayer-Petrov, in its September 2000 issue. The present translation was commissioned for this collection.

OLD WRITER FOREMAN

The left hand is itching like the devil. At the base of the palm, just above the wrist.

"This means money, God damn it!" says the old writer Foreman and gulps down the last drops of coffee from a paper cup.

"That would be very timely, Daddy," Peggy retorts.

"Where did I pick up Peggy?" Foreman asks himself and frowns, trying to remember where exactly it happened. The mental effort produces furrows that roll down his skull—hardened by wind and sun—like waves rolling across a sandbar. "Oh yeah! In Jamaica!"

He picked up the boozer Peggy in Jamaica about six or seven years ago. Or did she latch on to him? Back then he was still a pretty sturdy fellow—stocky and broad-chested, with mighty thighs, the square face of a Jewish longshoreman from Odessa and the bald skull of a Moscow safecracker. Foreman, however, had mastered a different trade. He had become famous by writing short stories, by inventing for each of them a vertiginous and unpredictable storyline. Why this striking resemblance to a longshoreman and a safecracker? It's because unlike poetry that soars upward on a winged Pegasus, prose lags behind in a cart drawn by a Budweiser horse. And because the safecracker's job of figuring out the locks' intricate codes is similar to the profession of a master storyteller, who has the intricacies of the plot at his fingertips. The brains of both the safecracker and the writer flare up from work, and their skulls expand.

He now clearly remembers that Peggy clung on to him in Ja-

153

maica. There she is now, the sassy blond, sitting across from her Daddy Foreman, chewing on the unexciting steak, dreaming of the cash that's about to start pouring into their pockets from the skies of New England. I'd kill for a drink, thinks Foreman and swallows his saliva, crushing the barren paper cup. But there's no way in hell! I barely have enough cash to pay for gas from here to the motel. What if they don't give me an advance at the *Newport Monthly?* thinks Foreman, and goes back in his mind to the time when he picked up Peggy in Jamaica.

Yes, in those days Foreman had both money and fame. That's why she latched on to him, even though she always claimed to have fallen head over heels. Nautilus Publishers in Boston had just put out a collection of Foreman's stories about a secret agent named Paul North, paying him a guaranteed advance of seventy thousand dollars in cash. This was unbelievable luck to Foreman after almost ten years of penniless and dormant existence in the land of the Soviets.

He had fallen out of favor in the old country after sending over for publication in the West the first of his stories about Paul North, which, by the way, had been rejected by all the "thick" journals in Moscow and Leningrad. The story was published in New York's finest magazine. Foreman instantly became a celebrity. Right away the *bastards* caught on to the fact that Foreman had made a leap into a different kind of fiction. He had turned an international spy who was working for the intelligence services of nearly all the great powers, including China and Israel, into an appealing romantic figure. At the same time, the spy was the enemy of the Soviets, hence a *negative character* by default. The story was deemed unprintable in Russia but received warmly in France, then Germany, Holland, England—and things started to take off. The *bastards* tried to force him to protest, to appeal to the international court of justice for an alleged violation of copyright, and meanwhile he used the same diplomatic channels (in Moscow he had a great number of diplomat friends) to send abroad his second story, then the third, the fourth, and so on . . . Finally the *bastards* offered him a writing trip to Jamaica. They told him it was all right if he stayed abroad for a while, enjoying the ocean air, knocking down coconuts and the like; the Soviet state, they told him, would not fall apart without him. In Jamaica, the contract with Nautilus Publishers was already awaiting his signature. Foreman went on a partying spree. In a month he was scheduled to go on a tour of American universities. By that time, the English translation of his book about Paul North was due to be released. The public's reaction to the book and its future success were in Foreman's hands.

To tell the truth, Foreman didn't want to be bothered with the financial side of the whole deal. There was so much money in his bank account that he could afford not to worry about it, at least for the next two or three years. Provided that his works would continue to be successful. He lived in an oceanfront hotel. He would get up early in the morning and clunk out three or four pages on his Olympia before breakfast. Then he would stretch out in a beach chair under the exotic canopy of a palm tree. He drank whiskey and soda—a habit he had acquired long ago in Moscow's diplomatic circles. He read trashy novels and contemplated his own new stories. He wanted to invent something completely unpredictable, like a game of soccer or a boxing match. And the field or the ring should most definitely be illuminated by the spotlight of a love story. Such stories were in high demand. The local publishing *sharks* were great suckers for these stories. The local *sharks* loved them, and the Soviet *bastards* hated them. That's why they never published Foreman's stories back in the Soviet Union. They loved to read his stories, but they hated him. The *bastards* hated Foreman, that is.

Foreman would slowly walk up and down the beach, kicking sea cucumbers with the tips of his sandals. These whitish penislike creatures would jut out of the sand, especially when he got nearer to the nude beach. Foreman loved kicking the cucumber so that it would fly up and plop down next to some wrinkled old doll with a spreading stomach and a withered little bush, or fly over the naked buttocks of a cooing couple.

One morning Foreman received an invitation to a cocktail party at the yacht club. A black Cadillac picked him up; the driver reminded Foreman of the drivers of those black cars that drove the *bastards* around or that the *bastards* used to send after a writer whose services they needed. Only the driver of the Cadillac was black—the drivers of those *bastard* cars were Slavs. The Cadillac was sent by Lord Roy Williams who at the time offered Foreman his patronage. At the yacht club Foreman picked up Peggy.

It was a motley gathering. The owners of luxurious yachts didn't shun the company of ordinary sailors. There were reporters, various rogues staying at local hotels, secretaries of embassies, rats—those Foreman could tell apart by their way of staring like pointers stalking the game. And as always at parties of this sort—flaky resort dames and professional whores. Foreman felt nauseous and lonely in this merry crowd. Every now and then Lord Williams introduced the Russian writer to some famous yachtsman, who turned out to be a publisher, a TV channel owner, an influential critic, or something or other of the sort. Out of politeness, Foreman would chat with them in his horrendous homegrown English, about his former trials and current success, and would be left to himself again. Walking around in circles, he eventually ended up in the poolroom. A tall aristocrat with a head of copper hair offered Foreman to play a game. The poolroom was empty, and this emptiness felt like fresh air after the suffocating reception hall saturated with sweat, alcohol, and perfume. The waiter brought them whiskey. Foreman and the aristocrat drank some and started playing. Only then did Foreman notice that in the corner of the poolroom, in a huge burgundy leather armchair, someone was napping. It was a blond creature, female, to judge by the dress and the red coral beads that had shifted to the side. On the floor next to the armchair, there was an emptied highball. That was Peggy. Foreman looked at her and immediately turned away, consumed by the game.

When Foreman sank several balls in a row and the copperhead aristocrat started nervously rubbing the end of the cue with chalk, Peggy woke up and demanded a new round of drinks. For herself and for the pool players. "I'm drinking to you, dear Foreman, because I love you," said Peggy, and kissed him. That's how she latched on to Foreman.

Peggy had come to Jamaica fifteen years earlier with her husband. They used to own a little shop at the hotel. Business was slow. They had no children. The husband went back to Liverpool. Peggy stayed behind, all alone, nothing but time on her hands. She was mad about books. She had dreamed of Foreman since she read his first story about Paul North. She had no doubt that Foreman was a genius, a superman. She sold her shop and went to America with Foreman. The first two or three years Foreman had both fame and money. They rented a luxury apartment in Cambridge, overlooking the Charles. Foreman was getting invitations to official dinners and fancy receptions. He lectured, met with the readers, toured the country. Peggy was always at his side.

Then the enthusiasm for Foreman's work started to fade away. Every day Foreman would lose one facet of success: he received fewer invitations, his stories were published with reluctance, and he received less and less money for them. The English translation of his second collection of stories was accepted by his publisher without much excitement. The first printing was small and didn't do well. Foreman and Peggy spent the advance in three months. Foreman started sending his stories to Russian émigré newspapers and magazines. They also published his stories reluctantly, paying very little and printing them with omissions.

He went on a bender, the way it used to happen to him in the land of the Soviets, in those bitter years of alienation from friends and persecution by the *bastards*. Peggy didn't lag behind. She kept up with Foreman in boozing and remained by his side.

At the peak of the second crisis, Foreman received a phone call from the editor-in-chief of the *Newport Monthly,* who invited him for a business chat. "We really need you, Foreman. The readers want your prose," he said to Foreman on the phone and scheduled the meeting.

That's how they ended up in Newport, Rhode Island, in this foul eatery with watery coffee and wilted steaks.

"Time to go to the editorial office," says Foreman.

"Are we walking or driving, Daddy?" Peggy asks.

"Let's just drag ourselves on foot. It's pretty close, thank goodness. If we drive, we'll lose the parking space. In this damned place, you'll die first before finding free parking," decides Foreman.

Foreman and Peggy walk uphill. They go past an ancient synagogue. They leave behind sturdy houses built one or even two centuries ago, by sea captains on the skeletons of murdered whales. They breathe heavily as they drag themselves up a hilly street toward an avenue of luxurious mansions, at the beginning of which stands the building of the *Newport Monthly.*

"God damn my old age and my poverty! Having to economize even on parking!" Foreman breaks down.

Peggy quietly minces at his side, wiping the sweat with the sleeve of a stylish turquoise shirt. All got up, the old broad! thinks Foreman, spitting off his saliva, brown from the Camel he's smoking. He leaves Peggy on a bench at the boulevard. He walks into the editorial office and announces himself to the secretary. He barely remembers how this happens, the negotiations with editors. How easy it is to forget, thinks Foreman, sitting in the waiting area. From the windows of the *Newport Monthly* he sees the roofs of the town.

Roofs sloping down to the harbor. Even though he can't see the water, Foreman knows that down there is the ocean, expanse, youth. He recalls the time when he sailed the seas, loved without restraint, drank carelessly and wrote his first sailing stories. Foreman looks out the window and sees the Black Sea, the Crimea, Sebastopol, ships on roadstead, and sailors cruising the evening boulevards with beautiful girls. He envisages his youth and wants to write a story about the expanse of the ocean and a whale in love with a submarine. Foreman laughs; the acuteness of the approaching plot tickles his nerves. He wants to sit down at his typewriter right away and start working.

The Editor walks out of his office. He has a sea captain's crimson face and a pastor's gold-rimmed glasses. He extends his arms as if to hug Foreman when they come together. Foreman walks toward him with arms open. They come together and energetically shake hands. Like an old friend, the Editor leads Foreman into his office, sits down next to him at the coffee table, and asks the secretary to bring in whiskey, vodka, gin ("Anything our dear guest would like!") and coffee. The indispensable coffee. They drink and snack on olives, and Foreman still thinks of sea, Sebastopol, and Peggy, with whom he would roam the city's nighttime embankment. The Editor and Foreman chat affably about writing, about sea stories. About true sea stories, where there is enough room for valor and love, the kind of sailing stories that practically nobody knows how to write these days, except the old masters like Foreman.

"Well, dear fellow, would you happen to have something suitable for our journal?" asks the Editor.

Foreman is thinking of sea, youth, and Peggy. Through fog his ship is slowly entering the harbor where she is sitting on the bench, his faithful Peggy. He feels a surge of pity and tenderness for her and he wants to open the window and call her. But the Editor keeps insisting:

"Something unfinished, perhaps? Notes, at least something that could be turned into a story. An idea, or something like that?"

"I have a story for you," replies Foreman tapping his bald skull with his right hand. "I do!"

"Give it to us! Send it!" the Editor entreats.

"The thing is, John"—the Editor insisted that Foreman call him by his first name—"the thing is that I still need to write the story down."

"What's the problem then, Foreman? Write it down, and we'll print it in the next issue."

"I need to spend a few hours at sea, John."

With his deep blue eyes sunk into their orbits, the Editor looks at Foreman. The Editor's crimson face breaks into an understanding smile.

"Why don't you go on a boat tour? For a whole day. Catch some fish. Breathe in some salt. And write your story."

Foreman hesitates. The Editor calls in the business manager and asks him to write out a check for Foreman.

"Here's your advance, dear Foreman. The rest—when the issue with your story comes out."

Peggy is waiting at the bench. Below there are three tiers of streets running down to the water. Foreman shows her the check for five hundred dollars. They go down to the harbor and find a box office that sells tickets for deep-sea fishing. They buy two tickets and go into the nearest tavern for a drink of gin and tonic.

"Your palm itched for the right reason, Daddy," Peggy says flirtatiously.

"You also have something itching, you sexy thing?" laughs Foreman and slaps her behind. "Still firm!" he thinks to himself, and smiles with pleasure.

They return to their rusty Chevrolet, leave the accidental parking space, and cruise the streets adjacent to the harbor until they find a decent motel. They dine at a nearby restaurant. They order thick chowder with shrimp and potatoes. They order fried fish, a huge bowl of tomato salad, and lots of beer. They relish the meal, smoke, drink coffee with blackberry cake, and return to their motel. They need to get some sleep. The fishing boat leaves at sunrise.

⌇

There is a line at the pier. Their boat, the *Poseidon,* rocks on small waves. The morning fog dissipates, making visible the sooty pipes and the ragged shell of the *Poseidon.* Peggy snuggles up to Foreman to stay warm. She cuddles up to him. Last night after dinner and beer they were "remembering Jamaica," as Peggy refers to it, for almost an hour. Still groggy, they are waiting to come aboard. Ahead of them in line is a youngish couple. Both with fishing rods, in overalls with hundreds of little pockets. Both of them recently retired and cheerful, they have just started to spend the money they had been saving their whole lifetime. The lady in navy overalls with pockets is very sociable.

"Did you get pills for motion sickness?" she asks Peggy.

"My wife loves any kind of motion," Foreman answers for Peggy, who is giggling in the face of the sociable lady.

They are now standing on the deck. They are issued fishing rods. They are asked to put three bucks each into the winner's pool. The cash prize will go to the luckiest one. Their spots are starboard. The *Poseidon* heads into the open ocean. Foreman feels good. He inhales the salty ocean wind and the rich mix of ocean smells. Peggy goes inside. Inside they sell beer and it doesn't smell like fish. Foreman feels good. The boat drops the anchor in a deep spot.

The fishing begins. Foreman puts a piece of squid on the hook and lets the weight unspool the line. Foreman sees how the fishing rod dances in his hands. He feels that the line becomes taut. He locks the spool and yanks the line—he strikes. Foreman reels in the line, pulling at and lifting up something heavy, fighting, alive, slapping the water with its tail. He drags the fish closer and closer to the deck. It's huge, with sharp predatory teeth and metallic lines along its torso. It gets harder and harder for Foreman to pull, and harder yet because he's afraid to lose this beauty, this once-in-a-lifetime gift of the ocean, this metaphor of fortune.

He yells for help, for someone to pick the fish up with a gaff, to get a net, so the fish won't get away. He yells with all his might, overpowering the choking pain that has appeared in his chest. Finally a sailor runs up to him and helps pull the fish on board.

Foreman has his picture taken with the fish, then with the fish and Peggy, then with the sailor, the fish, and Peggy, who is insanely proud of Foreman and downs a second can of Coors for the occasion.

"Maybe you've had enough fishing, Daddy?" says Peggy. "Let's go inside. You'll lie down."

She can tell that Foreman isn't feeling well. But he's not leaving the deck. He hooks a piece of squid again and puts the line in. The boat rocks slightly on the vertical waves. Up, down, and then a little to the side. "Dead hopeless ripple," thinks Foreman, looking at the water.

There's a lot of animation all around the boat. The fishermen and pulling out fish, one after another. But it's all small fry. "No way in hell, you sons of bitches. No way in hell! You can't beat an old sea wolf like myself!" Foreman thinks exultingly, even though he has no luck catching anything, and the cautious fish keep tearing the bait off the hook before he can yank. The ripple gets stronger. The pain in Foreman's chest mixes up with nausea. He sits down on a bench and leans against the bulkhead. The leftover squid is dangling off the banisters like a pendulum counting down the time of pain. Foreman looks at his watch. It's not even noon yet, and the *Poseidon* isn't due back in port until the evening.

There's no stopping the ripple.

There's no stopping the pain.

There's no turning the boat to the shore.

He who bites gets bitten, Foreman smirks, and I've jumped right at the hook.

Went on an ascent with mountain climbers. Made it out safely because I was healthy as a bull. And the heart wasn't failing me.

Asked to be transferred to a submarine and nearly ended up in a sea battle. Thank goodness the Suez crisis was over before long.

Flew to an expedition in a copter, which crashed onto a hilltop. Broke a few bones, but survived.

Fell in love with a long-legged singer, chased her all over Russia, and then she took off with a Brazilian conductor.

And here I'm now. Will I make it back to the shore? It hasn't hit me this bad for a while. And I don't even have my medication with me. Idiot!

Then Peggy resurfaces. Is she rocking because of the waves or the beer—who knows?!

"Darling, how's the fishing? These cretins are only getting small fry. The award is ours!" Peggy kisses him. From the stench of beer he feels even worse. But he doesn't have the energy to move away from her drunken caresses.

"Water. Bring me water," Foreman asks.

"Maybe beer, Daddy?" Peggy asks, unsure of what's going on.

"Water," repeats Foreman and leans back on the bulkhead.

The line with the bait has unreeled and gone to the depths. Foreman sees the rod jerk several times, but he can't force himself to get up, to yank, to bring it in. "Where has she disappeared to?" Foreman thinks about Peggy, who went to fetch water. He's waiting for water, resting against the bulkhead, with his mouth open. He inhales the nauseatingly warm air, rife with ocean rot and the beer the fishermen are pumping themselves with. Fishing is not great, nothing to write home about. But still, the day at sea is turning out pretty good! The beer's cold. Life's great. The old man got lucky. He will be champion. Except who would envy him, if he's sitting there on deck gulping air like a fish out of water?

Peggy returns with a can of lemonade. There's no water. On board there is everything one may ask for, except plain water. Who drinks water, when there's beer, coke, and lemonade! Foreman gulps the lemonade. The pain isn't going away. Peggy fusses about him, but it doesn't help. He drags his feet to the bow. There the air is clearer. The wind dilutes the repugnant smell of rotten fish, beer, and diesel fuel. Foreman sees a huge yellow cocoon of twisted thick rope. A hungry seagull is circling over the boat and screaming.

"I no longer have wings," Foreman says to the seagull. "I can freeze, go into pupation, crawl inside the cocoon. Go into a state of necrobiosis. I can disappear together with my pain. But it doesn't matter that I won't come out of the cocoon. As long as the pain stops."

He lies down on the yellow rope cocoon and tries to fall asleep. He falls asleep watching the sailor teach tipsy Peggy how to put squid on the hook. He falls asleep sliding along the metaphor of bait: some part of the swollen, wiggling, caterpillar-like red-necked sailor disappears inside a pulsating cocoon. A cocoon with Peggy's stomach in the middle.

Foreman wakes up to the wailing of music. The *Poseidon* is entering the harbor. Peggy shakes him, "Daddy, Daddy, we're back!"

She's wired. Foreman screws up his eyes: There're stripes on her neck and her chest, like those on the sailor's shirt. Stripes or love bites? But he shoves off the thought: Stupid nonsense! They're shadows of running clouds. Foreman gets up from the ropes. Around him there is a crowd: fishermen, wives, children. The captain comes down from the bridge and hands him a thick billfold.

"This is your award, Mr. Writer," says the captain. The public applauds, cheers, stamps their feet on the deck and whistles, congratulating Foreman. Peggy's very proud and doesn't even look in the direction of the sailor.

They walk down the steps to the pier. In her hands, Peggy carries a large plastic bag with the filleted fish that Foreman caught.

"I'm proud of you, Daddy," says Peggy and kisses him on the cheek.

"Then give this monster to somebody," says Foreman.

In front of them walks the same couple of the new retirees. Peggy catches up with them and hands them the plastic bag with the fish. The lady in the navy overalls tenderly hugs Peggy.

"Let's go have a drink, girl," suggests Foreman.

They stop at a tavern right in the harbor. The tavern is dimly lit and cold. The fan hums like a fishing reel. Foreman wants to dull the memory of pain and anguish. He orders two vodkas with tomato juice and spices—for himself and Peggy. Two Bloody Marys. Then two more. They leave the tavern, take a cab, and give the driver the name of their motel.

They shower, change, and go out. It's not dark yet, but the heat's gone. The sun is setting over the roofs of the stately mansions. Tourists roam the streets of Newport looking for a place to eat.

"You know what, girl, let's go to the best restaurant in town," says Foreman.

They don't know which one is the best, because they are in this seaside town for the first time. And there's nobody they could ask. Foreman doesn't like to ask. He prefers to push his way through like a bear. "You, Daddy, are like a bear. A real Russian bear," Peggy tells him in moments of tenderness.

They walk into a restaurant with a bar and a pool table. The restaurant is straight out of a cowboy movie. A gentleman in a wide-brimmed hat and denim shirt and the sailor from the *Poseidon* are playing pool. The sailor waves to them as if they were old friends.

They drink gin and tonic. They order oysters and a bottle of Frascatti. For dinner: turtle soup, lamb chops, and a bottle of nice Chianti to go with it. Then cappuccino. And chocolate torte with strawberries. Foreman feels almost back to normal. He drinks and eats plenty. He laughs at Peggy, who is dozing off and is not paying any attention to the sailor, even though he casts proud looks at her after every sunken ball.

From time to time Foreman looks at the large TV screen. A boxing match is on. A handsome black man in red silk boxer shorts wins the first two rounds. He corners his opponent, who is twice his age. Foreman thinks that he has misheard, misunderstood the pronunciation of the sportscaster, who is speaking with a strong Texan accent. But everything is correct. The old boxer, it turns out, used to be a famous champion, the *first glove,* as they say in Russian, the pride of America. But twenty years ago he lost his title. He became a coach and stopped fighting. "And then something incredible happened to him," the sportscaster intones. "The old boxer woke up one day and said to himself: I must return to the ring. I must. It's my life. My only calling. I don't want anything else!"

Foreman drinks his cappuccino and eats the chocolate torte. In the ring, it's the end of the third round. The young handsome guy continues to corner the old man, who looks like a bear: short, stout, with thick meaty cheeks, mighty torso, strong legs, and a brown shaved head. A typical longshoreman and a safecracker, just like me, thinks Foreman about the old boxer, who appeals to him. "Why did you get yourself into this, fool! Why did you get yourself caught on the hook?" Foreman asks himself or the other one, the one fighting in the ring. Whom?

He carries sleepy drunk Peggy back to the room, undresses her, like a little girl, brought home from a late party, the way God only knows how many years ago he used to undress his own daughter. He undresses Peggy, washes her face, puts her in bed, and she falls asleep all curled up. Foreman lies down next to her, but he can't fall asleep. You got enough sleep in the cocoon, he smirks. I just hope this thing doesn't fall through. Foreman thinks about the story he's supposed to be writing for the *Newport Monthly*. Something stirs inside him. Something is sprouting up. It's been a while since he wrote something really good. It's been a while since he felt the mysterious impulses, the underground jolts that make one dash to the typewriter and write, until the initial design becomes a story. Finished in its complete form.

He looks at Peggy. Nothing will disturb her. "Sleeping like a baby," thinks Foreman and turns on the TV. He lights a cigarette. The old boxer is having a rough time. He is defending himself, trying to protect his head from the long jabs of the handsome guy in red shorts. The old boxer is in green. It seems to Foreman that even the green of his uniform is faded, like grass at the end of August. The sportscaster quite openly roots for the handsome guy in red. For a second, the camera shows the sports arena and the front row of seats right near the ring. There—like a turned-off, dark spotlight— a female face in tears. Then the camera swiftly turns back to the ring where the young boxer is cornering the old guy. The old guy is defending himself; he doesn't try to attack. "Life is life," says Foreman with a sigh and turns the TV off. He feels sorry for the old bear, who resembles him so much. But what can you do! He shouldn't have gotten himself into this mess. He's already played all his cards. Can't go against fate! thinks Foreman and closes his eyes.

He lies in bed with his eyes closed. Peggy is breathing like a small child. He lies with his eyes closed and sees himself on board the *Poseidon*. He seems himself pulling out a huge striped fish and laying it on the deck in front of a roaring ecstatic crowd. He turns the TV back on and sees the ring. He can't quite figure out what's going on there, but he understands that an important change has taken place. The old man is moving faster than the young handsome guy, who's now forced to defend himself. But he's not trained for defense. He's only used to attacking. He feels uncomfortable in the corner, where the old man has forced him. He misses one serious jab after another: to the liver, to the head, to the chest. The referee stops the match, because the young guy's eyebrow is cut. The audience roars in excitement. The old man says something to his coach. The coach calls the referee over. The fight will continue until a knockout. The young boxer tries to attack. His jab goes between the old man's gloves. But that's a trap. The old boxer pulls back his head, making the handsome young guy lose balance and open up. The bear's left hand reaches his opponent's jaw. He goes down. The referee counts to ten. Knockout. The audience roars. Nothing like this has ever happened in the history of boxing. The referee lifts the old boxer's arm over the ring. The camera shows the face of the woman in the front row. She cries and laughs with happiness. Her face, like a black shining spotlight, illuminates the face of the winner.

Foreman falls asleep and dreams of a boxing ring floating in the ocean like a raft. He pulls his fishing rod over the ropes, casts, and catches big striped fish. One after another. The ring swims in the ocean and then moors to the shore. The rocky contours of the shore remind him of the profile of someone's familiar face. But he can't remember whose face or where the ring has moored. Sailors pull the ring out onto the shore. Those who wish to fight gather round. Foreman recognizes their faces. He used to socialize with them, drink vodka, trade gossip about writers. But he's completely forgotten their names, their gossips, their books. He doesn't know what to talk to them about, and throws the big striped fish over the ropes. They forget about challenging him to a fight, and start fighting among themselves over the fish. Foreman is fed up with all the fussing, and he pushes off and sails back to the open sea.

In the morning Foreman wakes up with the birds. Peggy is still sleeping, snuffling like a groundhog. He pulls the case with his Olympia out of the coat closet. He opens his briefcase and removes a stack of paper from it. He loads paper into the typewriter. Two sheets white as sea fog, with a sheet of carbon paper pressed between them. Like that young handsome boxer pressed into the corner of the ring. Foreman begins to write a story about the sea, a big fish, and a sailor who is in love with a waitress from a harbor tavern. In the story there is love, jealousy, murders, escapes, an insidious sheriff, and an incorruptible detective. Foreman spends the entire day writing. Peggy brings him coffee from a nearby restaurant. She tiptoes about the room. She's proud of her Foreman and anxious to know what the editor of the *Newport Monthly* will think of his new story.

Translated by Margarit Tadevosyan in collaboration with Maxim D. Shrayer

Composed in March 1995 in Providence, Rhode Island, "Old Writer Foreman" (*Staryi pisatel' Forman*) was published in the St. Petersburg monthly review *Neva* 12 (1998), in a special issue devoted to the works of Russian émigré authors formerly from St. Petersburg. The present translation was commissioned for this collection.

AFTERWORD

AFTERWORD
David Shrayer-Petrov,
a Jewish Writer in Russia and America

MAXIM D. SHRAYER

The dual name of David Shrayer-Petrov betokens his literary career. Born David Peysakhovich Shraer (Shrayer is an Anglicized spelling), he was descended from Podolian millers and Lithuanian rabbis. His father, Peysakh (Petr) Borukhovich Shrayer, an automobile engineer, came from an affluent Jewish family in Kamenetsk-Podolsk and was a naval officer during World War II. His mother, Bella Vulfovna Breydo, a chemist by training, came from the Broyda rabbinical dynasty of Šiauliai (Shavel) and Panevėžys (Ponevezh). As young people, both of Shrayer-Petrov's parents made the transition from the former Pale of Settlement to Leningrad (now St. Petersburg), where he was born on January 28, 1936. Growing up, Shrayer-Petrov heard Yiddish in the traditional home of his paternal grandmother. Evacuated from his native Leningrad in the late summer of 1941, as the Nazi siege closed in, he spent three years in Siva, a Russian village in the Urals. Folk rituals and the richness of peasant dialects left an indelible imprint on the writer's imagination. In 1944, the eight-year-old Shrayer-Petrov and his mother Bella Breydo returned to the devastated Leningrad. A Mediterranean-looking youth living in the city's

Vyborg working-class district, Shrayer-Petrov formulated the questions that his writings continue to probe to this day: Do Jews belong in Russia? Is assimilation impossible? Forty years later, in 1985–86, while living in Moscow and working on the first volume of his memoir-novel, *Friends and Shadows,* Shrayer-Petrov would apply these questions directly to himself as a Jewish-Russian writer: "Why do I not quote great Jews? I don't know the language. I only know Russian. . . . To understand the difference between Russians and Jews . . ."

Shrayer-Petrov started medical school in 1953, the year of Stalin's death, and entered the literary scene in the mid-1950s as a poet and translator of verse. He was one of the founding members of *Promka,* a literary seminar at the House of Industrial Cooperation, a group whose gatherings were attended by Vassily Aksyonov, Ilya Averbakh, Dmitri Bobyshev, Evgeny Reyn, and Leningrad's other young literary lights. In 1958, upon the suggestion of the poet Boris Slutsky, he adopted the pen name "David Petrov," the last name "Petrov" derived from Petr, the Russianized first name of his father Peysakh Shrayer. This assimilatory gesture hardly eased the publication of Shrayer-Petrov's poetry in Russia. His first poetry collection was derailed in 1964 following the trial of the poet Joseph Brodsky for "social parasitism"; it finally came out, in expurgated form, in 1967. During his Soviet years Shrayer-Petrov made a name for himself as a literary translator (especially from Lithuanian and the South Slavic languages) and an essayist.

Two years after his marriage in 1962 to the philologist Emilia Polyak, Shrayer-Petrov completed his Ph.D. at the Leningrad Institute of Tuberculosis and moved to his wife's native Moscow. His son Maxim was born in Moscow in 1967. By the early 1970s the relations between Jews and Gentiles became a principal concern of Shrayer-Petrov's writing. In 1975–76 he composed poems where the disharmonies of his aching Russian and Jewish selves adumbrate the writer's conflict with the Soviet system. In "Chagall's Self-Portrait with Wife," the poet asks the levitating Bella, Chagall's first wife: "Isn't there space enough / In that one-room hut to press / Your tired wings / Against his seething brushes /And love this country painlessly / All your life?" In "Early Morning in Moscow," the poet encounters a janitor who "shovels the street, / rehearsing his snowy reverie / *dirty Jew dirty Jew dirty Jew* / in the camps I'd break your head in two." Later the same day, a Jewish doctor comforts the poet as the echoes of the so-called Doctors' Plot of 1953 sustain the rhythm and meaning of the poem: "The doctor knocks on my chest / rehearsing his wishful reverie / *one day we'll one day we'll one day we'll* / be free to sing in the spring" (translated by Edwin Honig and Maxim D. Shrayer). Poems from Shrayer-Petrov's period of unsettlement circulated in *samizdat,* adding to the writer's publishing difficulties (many of them were later published in the West in his 1990 collection *Song of a Blue Elephant*).

In 1978, a scandal erupted following a televised reading at a poetry festival in Vilnius, Lithuania, where Shrayer-Petrov recited the controversial poem "My Slavic Soul." In it, unable to cope with the anxieties of a Jew who is culturally Russian, the poet's "Slavic" soul abandons his body, described as a "perennial, banal, so typically Jewish wrapping," and hides in a hayloft. The officials of the Union of Soviet Writers, to which Shrayer-Petrov had been admitted in 1976 with great difficulty and resistance from the organization's nationalist wing, threatened him with expulsion. The threat of ostracism for having transgressed the unspoken taboo on open treatment of Jewish subjects may have been the final draw, weaning the writer from his last illusions and pushing him to emigrate from the Soviet Union.

In January 1979 Shrayer-Petrov and his family applied for exit visas. Immediately fired from his academic position at the Gamaleya Institute of Microbiology and soon denied permission to emigrate,

Shrayer-Petrov became a refusenik. (The Russian term *otkaznik* means "the one who was *refused,* denied permission" to leave the Soviet Union. In its literal English translation, the term *refusenik* has acquired an ambiguity whose irony was hardly intentional: the Soviet authorities, not the Jews, were *refusing,* unless, of course, one also considers the fact that the refuseniks themselves had *refused* the ticket to Soviet paradise, some of them even renouncing Soviet citizenship). Following Shrayer-Petrov's expulsion from the Union of Soviet Writers, three of his books—a novel, a poetry collection, and a book of translations from Lithuanian—were removed from production, their galleys broken. Except for a few reprints of his translations, Shrayer-Petrov was unable to publish in the Soviet Union throughout his nine years of a refusenik's limbo.

In 1979–80, while driving an illegal cab at night and working at an emergency room lab, Shrayer-Petrov conceived of a panoramic novel about the mutilated destinies of Jewish refuseniks. *Herbert and Nelly,* one of the most significant and artistically compelling works to explore the massive exodus of Soviet Jews, awaits its English-language translator and readership. The novel exhibits a Tolstoyan sense of epic proportions in painting the lives of Jews from different walks of life sharing the plight of being Refuseniks and outcasts. The protagonist, Dr. Herbert Levitin, is a Moscow professor of medicine. His Jewishness evolves in the course of the novel from a prohibitive ethnic garb to a historical and spiritual mission. Levitin is married to Tatyana, a Russian woman of peasant stock, and their decision to emigrate ultimately results in the killing of their son in Afghanistan and Tatiana's own death of grief. In documenting with anatomical precision the mutually unbreachable contradictions of a mixed Jewish-Russian marriage, Shrayer-Petrov also treats the story of Dr. Levitin as an allegory of Jewish-Russian history. The Jews' marriage to Russia is doomed, the novels suggests to its Jewish readers. Emigrate or die! In book two of the novel, Palestinian drug dealers, chess, and sex fuel the plot as Dr. Levitin finds transcendent love in his new beloved Nelly but eventually perishes in his struggle with the Soviet system. The complete edition of *Herbert and Nelly* was published in the post-Soviet Moscow in 1992.

Soon after Shrayer-Petrov and his family requested permission to emigrate from the Soviet Union, the KGB unleashed a series of persecutory measures against the writer and his family, ranging from arrests and physical harassment to a smear campaign in the press. The persecution intensified in 1985, when the publication of the first part of *Herbert and Nelly* was announced in Israel (in appeared in Jerusalem in 1986 under the title *Being a Refusenik*). In 1985–86, denunciatory articles against Shrayer-Petrov appeared in central and provincial Soviet newspapers. Shrayer-Petrov was labeled a "Zionist" author and accused of "infecting" Soviet Jews with a hostile ideology. A real threat of being prosecuted, charged with anti–Soviet activity, and imprisoned hung over the writer and his family throughout 1985–87.

In spite of the persecution, Shrayer-Petrov's last Soviet decade was strikingly prolific. A refusenik's isolation from the rest of Soviet society, coupled as it was with the pervasive sense of the absurdity of being a Jewish writer who is both silenced by and shackled to Russia, led to Shrayer-Petrov's discovery of the prose form he calls *fantella.* One is tempted to decipher the author's coinage as "fantastical novella." How fantastical are these narratives? How fantastical are the Bible stories, Rabelais's *Gargantua* and *Pantagruel,* E. T. A. Hoffman's *The Devil's Elixir,* Gogol's *Nose,* Nabokov's *Invitation to a Beheading,* Bashevis Singer's *The Magician of Lublin?* In Shrayer-Petrov's *fantellas,* love, talent, and miracles oppose (and sometimes vanquish) totalitarianism and philistinism. In the title story of this collection, the *fantellic* gift of the Jewish composer-refusenik Jonah returns a long-lost son to the singer Sarah. "In the Reeds," the most overtly political story in the present collection, conjures up a bitter parable of perestroika through the eyes of a genius who rescues his beloved and his fellow dissidents by helping the inept *partocrats* to escape. Exile and lovelessness are the double price the protagonist of "In the Reeds" pays for his own freedom. In "Dismemberers" (1987), also included in this collection, Olympia the author's beloved typewriter continues to type subversive stories even after her owner has left Russia for good (the *fantella* was composed in Shrayer-Petrov's apartment while Dan Rather and a CBS crew were filming a fragment about him for the special *Seven Days in May*). Central to all three of these *fantellas* is the figure of a nonconformist Jewish artist clashing with the regime (the composer Jonah of the title story, the inventor Gulliver of "In the Reeds," the writer-narrator of "Dismemberers").

Leaving for the United States on June 7, 1987, Shrayer-Petrov brought with him a manuscript of the first of the two books of memoirs he would publish abroad. He insists on calling them "novels with the participation of the author," and they offer fascinating opinions about the making of Jewish writers in the Soviet Union (including a discussion of Joseph Brodsky's tangled Jewishness). Of *Friends and Shadows,* Victor Terras wrote in 1990 that "in its intellectual honesty and emotional ingenuousness [Shrayer-Petrov's] is indeed an 'open book.' " Emigration and an outwardly calm life in New England afforded Shrayer-Petrov both distance and perspective. Among the most celebrated works emerging from Shrayer-Petrov's American years is "Villa Borghese," part dirge, part confession of a Jew's expired love for Russia. Putting aside tortuously nostalgic recollections, the poet confesses that "For you and us, Russia, no closeness survives, / We sons of Yehudah who used to be yours" (this English translation by Dolores Stewart and Maxim D. Shrayer appeared in *Salmagundi* in 1994). As with other doctor-writers, such as Anton Chekhov in Russian literature and William Carlos Williams in Anglo-American, the writings of Shrayer-

Petrov are characterized by both analytical exactitude and passionate humanism. Notes of a Chekhovian treatment of a child's desperately literal—hence unmistakably truthful—vision of life's treacherous gray are particularly audible in "David and Goliath." A story of disorientation and transit, "David and Goliath" was composed in Ladispoli, Italy, where the writer and his family spent most of the summer of 1987 awaiting their American refugee visas. In a number of works, Shrayer-Petrov's scientific interests dovetail with those of a fictionist. The writer's lifelong research on bacteriophages and his investigation of the career of the great French-Canadian microbiologist Félix d'Herelle have informed his recent novel, *The French Cottage*.

Spanning two decades of Jewish themes and characters, this collection retrospectively showcases about one third of David Shrayer-Petrov's short fiction. In a number of stories written after coming to America—"Hände Hoch!," "He, She and the Others," and "Tsukerman and His Children" in this collection—love and marriage between Jews and Gentiles continue to fuel the imagination of Shrayer-Petrov the belletrist. Some of them gently ironic, others sharply polemical, the short stories about Jewish-Russian émigrés in America have become his form of popularity, and Shrayer-Petrov contributes to periodicals on both sides of the Atlantic.

Jews and Russians are the "two peoples [who] are the closest to me in flesh (genes) and spirit (language)," Shrayer-Petrov wrote in 1985, less than two years before emigrating from Russia. Rooting into his adopted land and its culture, Shrayer-Petrov features a greater variety of American characters. In three stories chosen for this collection—"Old Writer Foreman," "Hurricane Bob," and "Hände Hoch!"—as in the other recent fiction, Shrayer-Petrov inscribes his (autobiographical) émigré writers into the landscapes and culturescapes of his adopted country. Writing in Russian about the anonymity of American life, an anonymity that is both liberating and stifling, Shrayer-Petrov also assumes a greater role in the Englishing of his short fiction. Might he not wake up one day, magically equipped to write in English about his own America—Jewish-Russian, Russian-Jewish, ever unhyphenated?

Suggested Further Reading

Selected Books by David Shrayer-Petrov

Forma liubvi (Form of love). Moscow: Argo-risk, 2003.

Barabany sud'by (Drums of fortune). Moscow: Argo-risk; Tver': Kolonna Publications, 2002.

Zamok v Tystamaa (Töstemaa Castle). Tallinn: Aleksandra, 2001.

Frantsuzskii kottedzh (French cottage). Providence, R.I.: APKA Publishers, 1999.

Piterskii dozh (Petersburg Doge). St. Petersburg: Petropol', 1999.

Propashchaia dusha (Lost soul). Providence, R.I.: APKA Publishers, 1997.

Moskva zlatoglavaia (Gold-domed Moscow). Baltimore: Vestnik, 1994.

Gerbert i Nelli (Gerbert and Nelli). Moscow: GMP Poliform, 1992.

Villa Borgeze (Villa Borghese). Holyoke, Mass.: New England Publishing, 1992.

Pesnia o golubom slone (Song about a blue elephant). Holyoke, Mass.: New England Publishing, 1990.

Druz'ia i teni: roman s uchastiem avtora (Friends and shadows: Novel with the participation of the author). New York: Liberty, 1989.

V otkaze (Being a Refusenik). In *V otkaze,* 147–242. Jerusalem: Biblioteka Aliia, 1986.

Poeziia i nauka (Poetry and Science). Moscow: Znanie, 1974.

Kholsty (Canvasses). In *Pereklichka,* 115–60. Moscow: Molodaia gvardiia, 1967.

About David Shrayer-Petrov

Bobyshev, Dmitrii. "Shraer-Petrov, David." In *Slovar' poetov russkogo zarubezh'ia,* edited by Vadim Kreyd et al., 432–34. St. Petersburg: Izdatel'stvo russkogo khristianskogo gumanitarnogo instituta, 1999.

Gandel'sman, Vladimir. "Roman s uchastiem vremeni" (Novel with the participation of time). *Vestnik* 13 (1992): 32–33.

Katsin, Lev. "Kogo razdrazhaet boroda Tsukermana i pochemu. . . ?" (Who is irritated by Tsukerman's beard and why. . . ?). *Evreiskii mir,* 31 January 1997.

Lesnykh, R. "Raskaianie obmanutogo" (Repentance of the deceived one). *Fakty i argumenty,* 8 April 1986.

Lukšić, Irena. "Razgovor: David Šrajer-Petrov. Život u tri dimenzije" (Conversation: David Shrayer-Petrov: Life in three dimensions), *Vijenac,* 20 May 1999.

Sapgir, Genrikh. "Introduction." In *Gerbert i Nelli,* by David Shraer-Petrov. (Moscow: GMP Poliform, 1992), 3–4.

Terras, Victor. Review of *Druz'ia I teni* (Friends and shadows), by David Shrayer-Petrov. *World Literature Today* 64, no. 1 (1990): 148.

———. Review of *Moskva zlatoglavaia* (Gold-domed Moscow), by David Shrayer-Petrov. *World Literature Today* 69, no. 2 (1995):388–99.

———. "Roman ob otkaznikakh" (Novel about Refuseniks), *Novoe russkoe slovo* 28 Dec. 1992.

———. "Villa Borghese." *Novoe russkoe slovo* 3 July 1992.

Tukh, Boris. "Legko li byt' russkim pisatelem v Amerike?" (Is it easy to be a Russian writer in America?). *Vesti* (Tallinn), 22 Jan. 1999.

Parts of the Afterword originally appeared as "Shrayer-Petrov, David" in *Jewish Writers of the Twentieth Century,* ed. Sorrel Kerbel (New York: Fitzroy Dearborn, 2003), 534–36.

ABOUT THE TRANSLATORS

Thomas Epstein teaches humanities in the Honors Program at Boston College. A translator from French, Italian, and Russian, he has also published *Man and a Half,* a collection of his own short stories, and edited several books and anthologies.

Michael Fine is a family physician practicing in North Scituate, Rhode Island. He has published both fiction and nonfiction.

Dolores Riccio has published several books of nonfiction, including *Haunted Houses USA,* and several novels, including *Circle of Five.* As Dolores Stewart, her poetry has appeared in numerous periodicals.

Emilia Shrayer, David Shrayer-Petrov's wife of forty years, works at the Rockefeller Library, Brown University, and translates from and into Russian. Her translations into Russian with David Shrayer-Petrov include works by Erskine Caldwell and Australian poets. She translated into English David Shrayer-Petrov's *Staphylococcal Disease in the Soviet Union* (1989).

Diana Senechal is a writer of poetry, fiction, and songs, who is completing a collection of short stories. She translated from Lithuanian into English the poetry of Tomas Venclova for his book *Winter Dialogue* (1997) and edits the magazine *Sí Señor.*

Margarit Tadevosyan is a doctoral candidate in the English Department at Boston College, with a focus on Vladimir Nabokov and other multilingual writers. She has translated into English from her native Armenian and from Russian.

Victor Terras is Henry L. Goddard University Professor of Slavic Languages and Comparative Literature emeritus, Brown University. He has written and edited numerous books, including *Young Dostoevsky, A History of Russian Literature,* and *Handbook of Russian Literature.* Among his translations from Russian is Dostoevsky's *The Gambler.*